TEMPLE OF THE SUN

Other Books by Evelyn Sibley Lampman

TEMPLE
OF THE SUN

A Boy Fights for Montezuma

BY EVELYN SIBLEY LAMPMAN

Illustrated by Lili Réthi, F.R.S.A.

DOUBLEDAY & COMPANY, INC.

GARDEN CITY, NEW YORK

Library of Congress Catalog Card Number 64–16239
Copyright © 1964 by Evelyn Sibley Lampman
All Rights Reserved
Printed in the United States of America
First Edition

FOR LYLE AND DOROTHY JONES,
WHO LED ME BY THE HAND
THROUGH MEXICO

Montezuma's city, Tenochtitlán, was surrounded on all sides by the waters of Lake Tezcuco. The nearest neighboring cities were connected to Tenochtitlán by magnificent causeways, which stretched for miles over the huge lake. In the central plaza of the city stood the pyramid of the Great Temple, surrounded by smaller temples, the royal palaces, and other dwellings.

It is here that Chimal's story takes place. . . .

TEMPLE OF THE SUN

CHIMAL

TETEONI

ATOTOTL

MONTEZUMA II

CORTÉS

FATHER OLMEDO

ORTEGUILLA

DOÑA MARINA

I

"Stop! You have fought enough today!" called Ocelotl. His voice, coming from the shadows against the wall, was hoarse with age, and the words were spaced as though he had to form each one separately in his mind before he could chain them into a sentence.

The two boys who had been enthusiastically battling with small wooden swords, called *maquahuitls*, deftly fending off each other's blows with hard woven shields, let their arms fall to their sides obediently.

"It is almost time for dinner," announced Ocelotl, and the old voice sounded pleased. "Run home now, both of you. Come again tomorrow."

"But how did we do?" demanded Eecatl. He was the elder of the two boys, a thin, wiry twelve-year-old, whose only garment, a *maxtlatl*, or loincloth, tied around his waist and between his legs, was of coarse white cotton cloth. His hair was cut across his forehead, but left to grow long on either side and in back, and his bare, brown feet had never known or needed shoes, for they had grown protecting calluses of their own.

"If you had done badly I would have told you," snapped Ocelotl. For a moment he glared at Eecatl, and for good measure at Chimal as well. Then he relented a little, admitting, "You are coming along very

1

well. Someday you will be good warriors, which is not surprising, for I, Ocelotl, who was one of the greatest warriors in my time, have been your early teacher. Next month, the month of the Raising of the Quetzal Plume Banner, I shall recommend that you be admitted to the *telpochcalli*, the warriors' school."

Eecatl whooped with delight, and Chimal tried to produce a gratified smile for Ocelotl's benefit, but he felt a sudden heaviness inside him. The time he had always known would come was almost here, and he didn't want it to come, not now or ever.

Although Ocelotl spoke and moved slowly, his mind was keen, and now he looked into Chimal's face and his tone was incredulous.

"What is it, Chimal? You are afraid to be a warrior? Real battles are little different from the practices you have daily with Eecatl. He is a year older than you, and taller besides, yet you hold your own very well. Being a warrior for our country, Anahuac, is the greatest honor given to any of us. Tezcatli, god of the smoking mirror, will look after you when you serve under his banner. And if you should fall—although I cannot believe such a thing of a pupil of Ocelotl's—a warrior, whether he dies in battle, or under the sacrificial knife of the enemy, goes straight to the House of the Sun. He lives in a garden filled with flowers, and all day he fights sham battles such as you and Eecatl fight. When the sun rises in the east the souls of the warriors greet him with shouts of joy, and escort him across the sky." Old Ocelotl shivered with happy anticipation. He drew his cloak across his bare, crossed knees as he continued dreamily. "And after four years the souls of the warriors are changed into hummingbirds, and they feast all day on nectar. Even the souls of the enemy warriors go to

2

the House of the Sun. Who can ask for anything more wonderful?"

Eecatl looked at Chimal curiously.

"Don't you want to go to the *telpochcalli?*" he asked.

"Of course I do." Chimal tightened his *maxtlatl*, which, like that of his friend, was of white cotton, but of a finer weave, and prepared to step into his fiber-soled sandals that earlier he had left beside the wall. "I've always wanted to go there. I want to be a warrior like you, only I can't. I have to go to the priests' school, the *calmecac*. It's all arranged."

"Oh," said Eecatl sympathetically.

"Because you attend the *calmecac* instead of the *telpochcalli* does not mean that you cannot be a warrior," pointed out Ocelotl. "It means that you will be a leader of warriors, a chief. Most of our officers, save for the exceptional few who rose from the ranks by personal valor, went to the *calmecac*. It is the school for all young lords, and the training is very strict. I had forgotten that your father is a *pochteca*—a traveling merchant. He practices humility, so that it is easy to forget that he is next to the nobility."

"But you don't understand," insisted Chimal plaintively. "I'm to be a priest, not a warrior. I was dedicated to the priesthood when I was born."

"Plenty of time for that later." Ocelotl nodded his gray head, but his eyes had lost some of their former assurance. "You can be both—a warrior first, a priest afterward. Even the noble Montezuma, before he became emperor, was both warrior and priest. He led our armies to many victories, and later he served in Huitzil's temple. Why, the very day they came to tell him that he had been chosen to reign he was sweeping the pyramid steps."

3

"My uncle is high priest in the Temple of Coatlique," said Chimal in a small voice. "I do not think he will let me be a warrior. And I do not want to be a priest. Not for Coatlique, nor for any other god. They can't make me, either!"

"Chimal!" Eecatl gasped in alarm.

"Careful, boy, careful," warned old Ocelotl. "The gods will hear and punish you. We'll say no more about it. It is time to go home to dinner." He stretched out his two hands so that each boy could help pull him from the ground to his unsteady feet.

"Come tomorrow at the same time," he ordered over his shoulder. "And bring your *atatls*. If you're to leave me in a month's time you must have more practice in the throwing of darts."

Since Ocelotl had been such a valiant warrior and was now a pensioner of the realm, his tiny house was in the walled enclosure of the *telpochcalli*, the warriors' school, which Eecatl would enter in a month's time. It was a large establishment, with barracks-like buildings, glistening white in the sun, and surrounded by spacious grounds, most of which were utilized for training purposes. Targets were set up so that students could perfect their skills in bows and arrows, darts and javelins. Certain patches of ground had been worn bare by the feet of hand-to-hand combatants practicing with swords and shields. There were sections of ground given over to the manufacture of arms, for each prospective warrior must learn how to make his own, if need be. A dozen or so bows arched across racks to dry in the sun; mats, spread upon the ground, held the framework of round shields, partially laced with fiber and destined to be covered with feathers, mosaic, or metal ornaments; and there were piles of black obsidian,

4

to be chipped thin as a knife and used as the cutting edges of *maquahuitls* when the battles fought were no longer sham.

Usually when the boys left Ocelotl the grounds were crowded with students. Every target range was occupied, and young warriors thrust and parried with short practice swords, or bent low over the manufacture of arms. But today the square was deserted. Since Ocelotl had disappeared within his little house, they were the only two in sight.

"Where is everybody?" asked Eecatl in surprise.

"They must be listening to a lecture." Chimal ducked his head toward the large white building. The window openings were without glass, and by straining his ears he thought he could make out a single voice going on and on.

"Lectures!" Eecatl wrinkled his straight brown nose with distaste. "That's the one thing I'm not going to like about the *telpochcalli*. But at least they aren't given very often. Mostly we'll just learn to fight."

Chimal nodded soberly. At the *calmecac*, lectures were daily occurrences—lectures on astronomy, on poetry, on religion, on art, on etiquette, on picture writing and its reading, on interpretation of dreams and reckoning of years, and probably on a lot of other things he never knew existed. Not that lectures were so bad. Chimal didn't really mind them; it would be good to learn things. But there were other duties of a priest that he wouldn't like, things that he didn't even want to think about.

The *telpochcalli* backed up to one of the canals, as did most of the establishments and residences in the city. One could go any place in Tenochtitlán or its suburbs by boat, and usually the boat was tied up at a private doorway. Chimal's canoe had been left at the *telpochcalli* wharf, alongside all the war canoes belonging to the school. He got in, and Eecatl untied the hemp rope that held it to the piling, and jumped in afterward.

"I can hardly wait to tell my mother that I'll be leaving home soon," he said happily as they started down the canal.

"She may not be so glad to see you go," Chimal reminded him.

"Yes, she will. She wants me to be a warrior, and a good one. That's why she bakes tamales to sell in the market. The money goes to pay Ocelotl to teach me fighting skills before I'm ready for the school. My mother wants me to have a head start on the others."

"What does your father think about it?"

"I can do what I please so far as he's concerned." Eecatl shrugged. "But he'll be proud when I'm a hero. Maybe he'll wish that he had tried a little harder himself."

"Was he a warrior once?" asked Chimal in surprise. Of course he knew that everyone had to serve a term in the emperor's army, but it was hard to imagine Eecatl's good-natured, lazy father in a battle.

"Of course. But he wasn't a good warrior. It's just lucky that he wasn't taken prisoner. He likes things the way they are now," Eecatl told him cheerfully.

Chimal couldn't understand how this could be possible. Although there was no stigma attached to the position, Eecatl's father was a voluntary slave. He had sold himself to a rich man, and was now perfectly happy running errands. Neither Eecatl nor his mother shared the father's servitude, although they lived in the same house with him.

6

"I'll miss you when you go to the *telpochcalli*," he told his friend. "We've been together every day for a year, learning from Ocelotl. I won't know what to do with myself when we don't go there any more."

"You'll be away at school too," said Eecatl in surprise. "Will you go to the *calmecac* in the Great Temple at Tenochtitlán, or to the one here in Tlaltelolco?"

"I've told you that I'm not going," Chimal reminded him angrily. "I'm not going to be a priest—ever."

"We'd better talk about something else," said Eecatl hurriedly, glancing over his shoulder.

The canal was crowded with canoes, many of them filled with people headed for or returning from the *tianquez,* the market. The suburb of Tlaltelolco contained the greatest market in all the city, and at this hour the people in the canoes were buyers, for the sellers had gone early and would remain at the market until sundown.

Returning shoppers had their purchases with them: rolls of new matting, dishes of painted wood or clay, coils of rope, bags of maize or peppers or onions. Occasionally a live turkey gobbled a protest from a passing canoe, or there was the glint of gold and jewels as some great lady held up a new bracelet to be admired, and the sun peered at his own reflection in her purchase. Men, women, and children paddled the canoes with a skill that only comes with hours of daily practice, and a few were manned by slaves wearing wooden collars. Chimal couldn't help thinking that if Eecatl's father had to wear a wooden yoke about his neck he wouldn't enjoy his lot in life so much. But only the newly purchased or untrustworthy slaves were subjected to the wearing of this badge of servitude.

7

Eecatl had been still for some minutes. Now he spoke in a guarded tone.

"If you talked to your parents and told them how you really felt, maybe they'd let you start at the *telpochcalli* with me," he suggested. "At least they might let you go there for a little while."

"Maybe they might." Chimal brightened at the thought of a delay.

"That way you wouldn't be offending the goddess Coatlique. You could still be one of her priests someday, just as your parents promised. Only it wouldn't have to happen so soon."

"I'll talk to my father," declared Chimal eagerly. "He's away just now. He went to the sea coast to trade for amber and tortoise shell and jaguar and puma skins. He'll be home in another month, and I'll talk to him then."

"Will he let you?"

"I don't know," admitted Chimal. "It's my mother who really wants me to be a priest. Of course my father's proud that I can go to the *calmecac*, but sometimes I think he wishes they'd dedicated me to the warriors when I was born. Then, when there were no wars to fight, I could be a *pochteca* like he is."

"Why did they?" wondered Eecatl.

"My mother's brother, my Uncle Teteoni, had no sons. He wanted someone of his family in the temple, so he asked for me. And now that it's done he'll never let me off," complained Chimal bitterly.

"Don't say that," advised Eecatl, trying to make his voice hopeful. "Lots of things can happen." He got out at the boat landing where he lived, and Chimal paddled on down the canal to the section of Tlaltelolco that housed the merchants and their families.

9

Long ago these traders had grouped together in one area of the suburb where the canals opened directly onto the lake and where their boats could be brought straight to their warehouses built on pilings along the shore. Private homes were adjoining, with an open courtyard between and the whole enclosed by a protecting wall.

Chimal's father's warehouse was tightly shut today, but an old slave stood guard at the door. The boy waved as he dipped his right paddle to turn the canoe, and the slave bent to carry his hand from the ground to his head in a formal salute. It was old Cipactli, who had been with them as long as Chimal could remember and who was regarded as one of the family. Such formality was unlike him. Cipactli behaved that way only before strangers with whom he was impressed, and it took a great deal to impress him.

Then Chimal saw the canoe tied up at the landing, and he understood. It was painted black with green markings, for green was the color of nature, and there was an insignia of a broom on one side, with which Coatlique, the mother of the gods, could sweep the earth. A young priest in a stained black robe waited silently beside the oars. The sides and front of his head were shaved, but the crown was left long, and the straight black locks fell down over each shoulder.

Chimal tied his own canoe to the piling without looking again at the priest. He got out and crossed the wharf to the grassy patio beyond, deliberately scuffing his sandals against the rough boards. To drag or scuff one's feet was the height of bad manners, and it was the only way that Chimal dared vent his displeasure at this visit from his Uncle Teteoni.

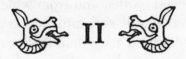 **II**

Because Ollin, the *pochteca*, was one of the richest of the traveling merchants of Tlaltelolco his home was quite large. There was, however, no display of wealth. Jewels and gold, exotic featherwork, embroidered cloth and rich furs, were kept hidden on the dark shelves of the warehouses and brought out only on market day or when the merchant was sure of a private buyer. For Ollin and his family to have lived in luxury or to have made a display of their own wealth would have brought the displeasure of the emperor. More than one merchant had been reduced to poverty, or even death, in this way. Only once a year, on their particular feast day, could the merchants wear jewels of gold and feathered ornaments and walk with their heads held high.

Comfort, however, was another matter, and the home that Chimal shared with his mother and father and his sister, Atototl, was very comfortable. Besides the warehouses there were several other buildings lining the sides of the open patio: the bathhouse, where steam could be introduced for a thorough cleansing; the kitchens; buildings for the use of the slaves; a separate spinning room for his mother and sister; and the main living quarters for the family. They were built of sundried bricks, painted white, and all of one story, for only the emperor and a few of the highest nobles were permitted two-story homes. Stairs led from the outside of the largest building to the flat roof, which was utilized as a second garden and from which the family could see over the wall and into the street below.

The courtyard within these buildings was green and grassy; water was carried from the canals to keep it so during the dry season. Woven mats were spread here and there, so that people could sit down, and there was no lack of pets: a pair of tame rabbits; a turkey, which had somehow managed to avoid the stewpot for so many years that he was now too old and too tough to eat; a beehive, tended by Atototl, who insisted that every inhabitant was her friend and that she could tell them apart; and two dogs, which belonged to Chimal, one large, with sad eyes, and one small and hairless.

The dogs heard the scrape of his sandals and came bouncing to meet their master and Chimal stopped to pet them before he turned in to the house. On the threshold he paused, adjusting his eyes from the brilliant glare of sunlight to the cool shadows of the room.

Three persons sat cross-legged on piled mats upon the polished flagstone floor. Before them was an open hearth, image and incarnation of Old God, the god of fire. Despite the warm day, two logs smoldered on the three sacred stones; for while the master of the household was on a hazardous journey the flame must be kept burning. In the corner of the room was a shrine to Yacatecuhtli, special god of merchants, before whose image incense curled in a thin blue streamer, and on a low table made of woven reeds a vase of bougainvillaea made a coral splash against the white walls.

Mazatl, Chimal's mother, glanced up and saw her son standing in the doorway.

"Ah, here you are," she said. "As you see, we have a guest, your honored uncle, and his time with us is short. Often Ocelotl keeps you late, so I thought it better that we start our meal without you."

Chimal smiled quickly at his mother to let her know that he understood. Then he bent to carry his hand from the ground to his head in a respectful salute to his uncle, the high priest.

Teteoni was rather a frightening man to look upon. The sides of his head were shaved like those of the young priest in the canoe, but the black hair that fell down from the crown was tangled and matted. His long black robes were embroidered with blood-chilling symbols, and Chimal was sure that they were never washed, for they always gave off an unpleasant odor. The priest himself, however, was clean, for twice a day and at least once during the dark hours of the night he was required to bathe in the icy waters of the temple pool. His face was scarred from self-inflicted penance with agave and maguey thorns, and his tall body, beneath the soiled robes, was thin and gaunt from many fasts.

Since this was not one of his fast days he was eating as fast as he could, stuffing tamales filled with fruit into his mouth one after another.

Tochtli, a little maid, brought Chimal water in a bowl to wash his hands, then a small dish filled with white fish cooked with peppers and tomatoes. Teteoni, who had already finished a large helping of fish before starting on the tamales, regarded his nephew disapprovingly.

"You spoil the boy, Mazatl," he told Chimal's

mother. "That food is too rich for children. Maize cakes, that's what he should have, and the girl too. Let's see, how old is he now? Ten? Then one and a half maize cakes three times a day should be his regular diet."

"He needs more than that, brother," Mazatl told him apologetically. "He is still growing. Besides, Chimal is eleven now. Almost twelve. And Atototl is past thirteen. One and a half maize cakes would not be enough."

"Two then," agreed Teteoni grudgingly. "That's what our students in the *calmecac* get at each meal. Except on fast days, of course. So Chimalpopoca is eleven now? You should have told me. The years slip by. It's time he was entered in the school. It takes years of preparation for the priesthood. I could take him back with me today, if you like."

"No!" cried Chimal loudly.

"He's been studying with Ocelotl," explained Mazatl quickly, frowning at Chimal because he had raised his voice. "Perhaps we should wait until his father returns. It will be only another month."

"I'll feel much better when we get him in the *calmecac*." Teteoni shook his head soberly. "These are perilous times, sister. The signs have been bad, very bad."

"What sign?" asked Atototl curiously, forgetting that she should not speak unless asked a direct question by a priest, even if he was her uncle.

Teteoni was not offended. He enjoyed the subject, and welcomed an opportunity to speak on it at length.

"Signs have been appearing for a long time," he began somberly. "I was one of the first to notice them. I called them to the attention of the high priests of the Great Temple of Huitzil and Tlaloc. First, the great lake of Tezcuco, without earthquake or tempest

14

of any kind, overflowed its banks and poured into the city of Tenochtitlán. It swept off many buildings, you remember."

"No," said Chimal thoughtfully. "I don't remember."

"It happened nine years ago," Mazatl explained softly. "You were only two years old, and Atototl was four."

"What are nine years to the gods?" asked Teteoni scornfully. "It was the beginning, the first sign. Then, a year later, one of the towers of the Great Temple caught fire, also without cause. It continued to burn until nothing remained but the stonework, despite every attempt to put it out. That was the second sign."

Chimal lifted his eyebrows at Atototl, who shook her head. She didn't remember that incident either.

"After that there were three comets seen in succeeding years," continued Teteoni, warming even more to his subject. "And everyone knows that they are omens of misfortune. The stars are gods, and when they stray from their rightful places and start moving across the sky they foretell doom. Then there was that strange light in the sky. I'm sure you can remember that. It was in the month of the Stopping of the Water."

This time they all nodded seriously. There had been a strange light in the night sky early that year. It had been shaped like a pyramid, broad at the base and tapering to a point. It resembled a pale fire, and sometimes it seemed to give off sparks. A few people claimed to have heard low voices and doleful wailing at the same time, but try as he would, Chimal had never been able to hear anything.

"And then," finished Teteoni triumphantly, "Popocatepetl has just erupted. During the month of the

15

Return of the Gods it could be seen all over the city. Old Popo always warns her children."

"Of what?" asked Mazatl fearfully. "You are a priest, brother. What does the lady Coatlique tell you about these signs? What is going to happen?"

"The goddess is silent," admitted Teteoni. "Even to me, she will not divulge the meaning of these things. But one thing I do know. We are in the year Ce Acatl, One Reed. And the year of One Reed was when Quetzalcoatl, god of wind, life, and morning, god of the plumed serpent, promised to return to Anahuac."

"Do you really think that's what it means?" Atototl's voice was more curious than frightened.

"Yes." Teteoni nodded. "I do. I think that Quetzal is returning as he promised he would. That is why I want Chimal to enter the *calmecac* quickly. Quetzal is the patron of that school; the young men of the *calmecac* belong to him. I want Chimal to be among them."

Chimal thought quickly. Quetzal was a great god. He was good and benevolent, and he loved men. Unlike the other gods, he had a fair skin and blond hair, with a great golden beard that covered his chest. He was a friend to the Aztecs, and had led them here hundreds of years ago and shown them how to build this city on the lake. Before he was driven away by the other gods he had discovered corn, hidden by ants in a hill, and had taught men how to find and polish jade and other precious stones. He had taught the women how to weave multicolored fabric from cotton, and the men how to do mosaic work with the feathers of the quetzal bird, the parrot, and the hummingbird. It was Quetzal who had taught men science—how to arrange the calendar, and study the movement of stars, and to measure time. He had devised the ceremonials and

16

fixed the days for prayer and sacrifice—only Quetzal didn't believe in human sacrifice. He loved men too much for that. Perhaps it would not be so bad to serve a god like that if he returned. He was not like the others.

There were sudden noises outside in the courtyard. Someone was coming, for both dogs had begun to bark, and the turkey, who had come to consider himself the third watchdog, was gobbling loudly. A second later the sunlight was blocked from the doorway and Atototl, who was closest, had scrambled to her feet.

"Father! Father!"

Ollin, the trader, was dusty, and the *tilmatli*, a cotton cloak which he wore from his shoulder, was tattered and so soiled that it could no longer be called white. He must have traveled fast, for the scant beard that he scrupulously shaved each day straggled over his chin.

"Ollin!" cried his wife in delight. "You are a month early. We did not expect you. And you come in broad daylight, not at night, and secretly, as you usually do."

The merchant made obeisance to the shrine of Yacatecuhtli and formally greeted the high priest before he began embracing his family.

"This time there was no need to arrive secretly," he told them. "I left my goods for Tecpatl to bring on while I hurried to the emperor with news."

"The emperor? Montezuma himself?" Mazatl gasped. "You are going to see the emperor? To talk with him?"

"I have seen him," Ollin told her. "My news would not wait."

"What news was that?" asked Teteoni eagerly. "Or did His Majesty pledge you to silence?"

"It wasn't news after all," admitted Ollin ruefully. "At least, not to Montezuma. His Majesty already knew of it, as he knows of everything. But he was gracious enough to commend me for trying to warn him. By the day after tomorrow the whole city will know, so it's no secret. There are men with white skins marching this way. They wear clothes of shining silver, with plumes in their headdresses. And they ride upon strange, monster beasts, the like of which I have never seen. They arrived in great water-houses from across the sea, and they have vanquished our enemies, the Tlascalans, who are now their allies and march with them. On the way they burned our holy city of Cholula, because its people dared to stand against them, and unless Montezuma acts quickly they may do the same to us."

"Tell me," demanded Teteoni, and his black eyes glittered wildly in his scarred face, "one of these men with a white skin, did he have a long golden beard?"

"Why yes," agreed Ollin after a moment. "He did. I saw it at Cholula when he removed his headpiece."

"Fool!" snapped the high priest. "Don't you know who he is? He is no enemy. It's Quetzalcoatl himself, returning to his home as he said he would."

III

It was scarcely light when Chimal untied his canoe at the landing, but although he was early, he was not the first. Ahead and behind, other canoes were beginning to form a straggling procession. They were bent, as was he, on arriving at a vantage point where they could get the earliest view of the white-skinned strangers. In another hour the canal would be choked with watercraft carrying people to either side of the great dike of Iztapalapan, which stretched in a straight line across the salt floods of Lake Tezcuco to the city gates.

Several drawbridges spanned the giant causeway, and Chimal and Eecatl had agreed that they would await the arrival of the strangers at the first bridge. Tenochtitlán covered a lot of ground, twenty-five-hundred acres in all, and it would take even a god a long time to march from the outskirts to the Palace of Axayacatl, which had been prepared for his habitation.

Tonatiuh, the sun god, had not yet made his appearance, but the eastern sky was glowing red with the lusty shouts of his herald warriors. The waters of the canal were black when Chimal's paddles dipped below the surface, and the canoe itself was filled with shadows that somehow seemed deepest in the prow. Chimal squinted at those shadows thoughtfully, wondering if he had forgotten and left his other *tilmatli* in the canoe last night, or if someone had dropped something there, a roll of matting or a length of cloth. Then, surprisingly, the knot of shadows began to move, and Chimal's heart pounded loudly, fearful that one of the dread night spirits was waiting to snatch him away in this last second before the protecting eye of Tonatiuh had cleared the horizon.

"Hello," said a familiar voice, and Atototl's slight form evolved from the shadows and sat up in the canoe.

Chimal was very angry, even more so because a moment before, he had been frightened.

"What are you doing here?" he demanded. "Why were you hiding in my canoe?"

"Because I'm going with you," announced his sister cheerfully. "And I knew you wouldn't take me if I asked."

"I won't take you now. You're supposed to watch from the rooftop with Mother. Eecatl and I don't want a girl hanging around."

"Eecatl won't mind," Atototl told him airily. "Keep on paddling, stupid. Do you want to be rammed in the dark by a canoe?"

"You can't go," objected Chimal again. "You're a lady. You can't hang over the edge of the causeway like a boy or the daughter of a common person."

"Who will know who I am but you and Eecatl? There's sure to be a big crowd. If I see someone we know I'll hide. I want to see Quetzal too."

"You can't see him with us."

"Of course I can," insisted Atototl. "And if you stop to take me back you'll be so late that you won't get to the first drawbridge. Here's Eecatl's landing. You'd

21

better turn in while you can. You'll never be able to turn around in this line of canoes."

Chimal ground his teeth in rage, but turned the canoe in to the landing spot. Atototl was right. There was no time to take her home now. But there was some comfort in knowing that when Mother and Father discovered what she had done, she'd be reprimanded. She'd be pricked with agave thorns, and perhaps she'd have to inhale burning pepper fumes besides, for these were the usual punishments given Aztec children who misbehaved.

Eecatl was not nearly so disturbed as Chimal on finding that Atototl had joined them.

"But you'll have to look out for yourself," he warned. "We won't have time to boost you up the dike and make sure you don't slip."

"Don't worry about me," said Atototl. "I wore an old skirt, one that I had before Mother decided I should start letting them down. This one comes to my knees. I can climb anywhere you can."

"And make a spectacle of yourself doing it," said her brother.

Before long it grew light enough so they could see. Looking back over his shoulder, Chimal wondered what Quetzal—if it was Quetzal—would think of the changes wrought in his city since he had gone away. They had left the suburb of Tlaltelolco behind, and now they were skirting Tenochtitlán proper. Towering above the flat rooftops was the great double pyramid of Huitzil and Tlaloc in the temple square, and behind that, like a supporting army, marched the lesser pyramids of the other gods of Anahuac. From this distance it was impossible to see the bright banners, intricately woven of blue and green, yellow and crimson feathers, or the precious jewels, set in carvings of gold and used to decorate the temple atop each pyramid, for the heavy incense burning in half a hundred golden braziers wrapped each peak in a gauzy layer of smoke.

The canoe skimmed under one of the great draw-bridges, which could be raised or lowered at will. Now they were passing a section of the city that housed many of the lesser nobility. The canal was narrower here, for half its former width was given over to a street covered with hard cement. Sweepers were already working with brooms and clay pots of water, a daily ritual that kept the streets of Tenochtitlán glistening white and spotless.

Although the residences were of a single story, their porticoes were embellished with porphyry and jaspar, and the rooftops were bright with garden flowers and low-growing shrubs. A few balustrades had been hung with fresh-made garlands, and these, Chimal knew, belonged to people who believed that the white-skinned strangers were gods.

To his amazement this view was not shared by everyone. There were those who feared that the newcomers were warriors bent on conquest, and they questioned the wisdom of admitting them within the city gates. Chimal's father was one of these. He had seen the destruction by the strangers of the holy city of Cholula; he said they were not gods, but warlike men. Teteoni thought otherwise, and he, a priest, should be wise in such matters. Chimal had decided to reserve judgment until he had seen them for himself. Perhaps there would be a sign given, so he would know.

Atototl and Eecatl were chattering happily in soft voices, delighted to be abroad on this adventure.

"What I want most to see," declared Atototl, "are the magic beasts that belong to these strangers."

"Why do you think they're magic?"

"They must be, because no one has ever seen their kind before. Father says they walk on four legs, like ocelots or jaguars, but their tails are like a woman's hair, long and silky. They have hair on their necks too, but not on their heads. They're very big, and the strangers ride upon their backs. And these beasts wear clothes."

"Clothes?"

"Ornaments too." Atototl nodded, delighted at the impression she was making. "Made of shining silver. And their mouths are filled with silver chains."

"I don't see how they can eat with silver chains in their mouths," objected Eecatl.

"Maybe they don't need to eat," decided Atototl. "After all, if they're magic, eating may not be necessary."

By this time the canal was filled with canoes, all heading south. They made a procession, a sold dark line, two and sometimes three abreast. The street was beginning to fill with people, and on the rooftops families were gathering, although it would still be some hours before the strangers could progress this far. There was no shouting or boisterous conduct, for the code of Aztec manners frowned on loud voices and riotous behavior.

Eventually they came to the last of the drawbridges, and here Chimal's skill as a boatman was really taxed, for they were no longer in the clear waterways of the canal but in the lake itself, and surrounded by *chinampas,* the wandering islands upon which the ancient city had been built.

Quetzal would feel at home here, Chimal thought, paddling quickly to avoid a slow-moving mass of green growth. When the god had led the Aztecs here, so many years ago, he noticed the masses of earth loosened from the shore and floating free on the sluggish waters of the lake. He had told the people to build rafts of reed and rushes, and these had formed bases for the rich sediment that they drew up from the bottom of the lake. On these floating islands were grown unfailing crops, maize and vegetables and flowers, and after a while some of the *chinampas* became so firm that they would support even small trees. They were still the richest producing gardens in all the city.

Chimal maneuvered his canoe into the last remaining space against the dike, and Eecatl managed to wind the rope around one of the rough stones from which the dike was built. It had been cold when they set out, but now that the sun was rising higher in the sky it grew warm. It was long past breakfasttime, but no one had remembered to bring food. The odors of cooking that floated over the lake from the little huts on the *chinampas* made them even hungrier, but that was forgotten when they heard the sounds of approaching music. At least Chimal thought it was music. It was high and melodic, but no conch shell, no clay whistle or reed flute could have produced such notes.

People in the canoes tied to the dike began climbing up the stones. Eecatl was out first, with Chimal close behind. Atototl tucked up her skirt in front, so that she wouldn't trip, and followed.

No one presumed to stand upon the causeway itself. The moment each man's eyes were able to see over the top, he stopped climbing, clinging tightly to the

stones. Chimal thought how funny all these bodi-
less heads must look to anyone walking along the road.
Then he forgot about the impression they might make,
for he realized that music was also coming from the
opposite direction. This time it was made by instru-
ments that he recognized, the royal conch shells,
heralding the arrival of the emperor. Montezuma himself had left the palace to greet these strangers, and
that meeting must be going to take place right here.

"It's the emperor," whispered Eecatl in alarm.
"What should we do? We can't bow and touch the
ground—not and hang onto these rocks."

"Maybe he won't come this far," Chimal told him
hopefully. "Maybe he'll stop before he gets to the
bridge."

"Look!" Atototl's voice rose in excitement. "The
magic beasts!"

As the vanguard of strangers appeared at the end
of the bridge a low moan of fear came from the rows
of heads lining the causeway. The Aztecs had no beasts
of burden. Many of them thought these men and
mounts a single, terrifying animal, sent by the gods as
punishment for a sin.

Since Ollin had prepared them, Chimal, Atototl, and
Eecatl did not make this mistake, but they stared at
the animals with curious amazement. They were huge:
twice—no, three times—the size of the largest jaguar
Chimal had ever seen. They were covered with short
fur, and some were white, some black, some reddish-
brown. Their long, drooping tails were indeed like the
unloosened hair of women, and blew gently in the
breeze. The animals wore glittering silver blankets that
covered their backs and reached well down on each
side, and silver headdresses extending over their arched

necks. But Atototl had been wrong about the purpose
of the silver chains in their mouths. They were not for
decoration alone, but ended in leather straps, the ends of
which were held by the rider.

Chimal let his eyes travel up the reins to study the
riders. They too were dressed in shining metal, which
glittered and sparkled in the sun. It encased their
whole bodies and covered their heads like bonnets.
These were decorated with plumes, white or red,
black or azure blue; but the birds that grew such
feathers were not to be found anywhere in Anahuac.
Each stranger carried in his gloved hand a long lance
with a bright cloth pennon attached, and dangling
from his side was a gigantic knife, almost as long as
his own body. It was made not of wood but of the
same metal that formed his clothing.

The riders had been advancing two by two, and just
as the leaders reached the point in front of Chimal,
one of them held up a gloved hand and the whole
procession stopped. He had seen Montezuma's ap-
proach from the other end of the bridge.

From the rear of the procession a man ran forward.
No doubt he was one of the common foot soldiers,
Chimal decided, or perhaps a slave, for he wore no
silver garments, only a padded jacket and leggings
of cotton. His head was covered by a plain metal cap.
He helped the leader to descend from his mount,
jerkily, and with loud, clanking noises, and while he
stood there on the causeway Chimal was able to see
him more clearly.

The metal headpiece was open in front, and
through this space a face was visible. It was thin, un-
smiling, and the skin was pale. A scant dark beard
showed on the cheeks, and as soon as he saw this,

Chimal knew that the stranger was not Quetzal. Quetzal was fair and golden-haired, and his beard was long and curling.

The stranger stood there quietly waiting, his face calm, his head in its crested bonnet looking straight ahead, while Montezuma's party advanced slowly toward him.

"What shall we do?" whispered Eecatl frantically.

"Stay where we are," advised Atototl. "Nobody's going to look at us."

By twos and threes the heads were disappearing from the top of the causeway. People who had dared to look upon a possible god were afraid to lift their eyes to the emperor. Common folk were expected to prostrate themselves upon the ground in his presence, while nobility bowed their heads and looked down when he passed by.

Chimal unhooked his chin from the surface of the causeway and lowered himself a foot or two against the dike. Everyone else was clinging in a similar fashion, nose pressed to the stones. Chimal felt his anger rise against his emperor as he thought of the injustice: people had risen early, and paddled fast and long for this first view of the strangers. Now it had been snatched away because Montezuma hadn't been content to await their arrival in his palace, where he belonged. The boy ground his teeth with frustration and looked at Eecatl, clinging to the rocks beside him, expecting to share the disappointment. But Eecatl had closed his eyes in additional reverence to his monarch. Chimal looked past his friend to Atototl, and shook his head with disbelief. Atototl alone, of all the watchers on the dike, had not lowered her body from its original position. Her chin still rested on the causeway, and she was still observing.

Chimal's first impulse was to speak sharply, to remind his sister of her manners. What must people be thinking of her? He leaned out and peered at the figures clinging to the dike. To his surprise, no one else seemed aware of Atotol's conduct. Like Eecatl, many of them had closed their eyes; others were patiently waiting, their cheeks against the brownish-gray stones, until the emperor had finished his business and gone away.

But if Atotol was unobserved by the common people she could not hope to escape the eyes of Montezuma's nobles, walking along the causeway. One of them was sure to glance over and see the small, shining head, black against the white pavement.

Chimal spoke her name softly, and Eecatl opened his eyes and said, "Sh" in a reproving whisper before he closed them again. Atotol did not even hear him, and Chimal realized that he would have to climb back up to attract her attention. The moment he reached the top he forgot his mission, for Montezuma's dazzling retinue marched straight into his line of vision.

First came three officers of state, richly dressed, but with bare feet, and carrying golden wands. Behind them followed the royal palanquin, or litter, so blazing with gold that it made Chimal blink. It was set with royal turquoise, and was carried on the shoulders of four high-ranking nobles, who were also barefoot, to show humility in the presence of their sovereign. Within the palanquin reclined Montezuma II, and above his head was suspended a canopy made of featherwork mosaic, embroidered with turquoise, and carried by four more barefoot nobles. The whole procession walked slowly, eyes turned downward. No one looked to left or right, and Chimal realized with pleased astonishment that he and Atototl were perfectly safe. At a time like this the nobles would not waste glances at the familiar causeway. Any sly peeks would be for the white-skinned visitors. He prepared to enjoy himself.

The white leader seemed undecided about his own role in this meeting. His mail clanked and jangled while he took a few steps forward. Then he must have changed his mind, for he stood still, waiting for Montezuma to come to him.

When they had reached a spot a few feet away the cortege stopped and the four nobles carefully put down their burden. Montezuma stepped out, and two men rushed forward to assist him. Chimal recognized them both. One was Cuitlahua, Lord of Iztapalapan, and Montezuma's brother; the other was Cacama, Lord of Tezcuco. There were not two more distinguished nobles in the realm.

As the three walked slowly forward the other attendants strewed the causeway with cotton tapestry, so that their emperor's golden sandals would not come in contact with the paving.

Chimal had never seen his ruler so close, and he knew that he never would again. He made the most of the opportunity.

Montezuma was tall and slender. Across his shoulder was a *tilmatli* of the finest cotton, intricately embroidered with pearls, emeralds, and turquoise. On his head was a *panache,* a headdress of royal green plumes from the quetzal bird, and around his arms and ankles were bracelets of gold, set with precious stones.

Matching jewels flashed from his ears and from the plug thrust through the cartilage of his nose.

The two men, emperor of the Aztecs and leader of the white-skinned strangers, were facing each other now, and Chimal heard his monarch's voice speaking the old words of courteous greeting.

"Welcome, Malinche. Welcome to my city of Tenochtitlán. May your visit with us be filled with happiness and joy. May the gods smile upon you and upon us, their people."

Malinche! Chimal's sharp ears picked out the form of address. So that was the stranger's name. It would be known to Montezuma, of course. His spies were everywhere, and they kept him informed on all matters.

Malinche replied to the welcome in a deep, resonant voice, but the words were strange and unrecognizable. Even Montezuma was at a loss, and the visitor smiled and waved his hand. A few seconds later a woman came hurrying forward. She was small and pretty, and her black hair was braided with ribbons and wound around her head. She wore a native skirt made of a single length of cloth, wrapped around her body and tied at the waist by an embroidered belt, and an embroidered overblouse of fine cotton. Jewels sparkled in her ears, and her arms were loaded with bracelets. But unlike the men with whom she traveled, her skin was the color of shining copper. She was an Aztec, and one who had been well versed in manners, for she made the proper obeisance to the emperor before she spoke.

"My lord Malinche thanks you for your welcome, sire," she said finally. "He bids me tell you that he comes in peace to bring greetings from his master, the greatest king of all the world, Charles of Spain, who lives across the sea. He also wishes to tell you of the true religion, and of the one god who rules over us all."

For a moment Montezuma almost forgot the courtesy due a guest. He frowned, then recovered himself.

"Tell Malinche that I have heard of no king greater than Montezuma," he said finally. "And as for his god, tell him that we have our own. They serve us, as we serve them. We have no need of others."

The woman translated this speech rapidly into the strange tongue, and when she had finished Malinche spoke again.

"My lord says he will enlighten you further on these matters at a later meeting, sire," said the woman. "In the meantime he asks that you accept this necklace of stones from another land as a small token of his esteem."

The necklace was of brightly colored beads, and when it had been placed around Montezuma's neck the stranger moved forward with outstretched arms as though to embrace the emperor. Instantly the nobles stepped between, and Chimal gasped with horror. No one must touch the person of the emperor. The woman spoke softly, warningly, and Malinche laughed, saying a few words that she translated.

"My lord Malinche meant no offense, sire. In his country the person of the ruler is not so sacred as it is here. Their king may be touched by mortal hands."

But Montezuma was taking no chances. He was back in his palanquin, which immediately was raised to the shoulders of his nobles. The glittering procession moved quickly away, and only Lord Cuitlahua remained.

"His Majesty bids me escort his guests to the Palace

of Axaya',"" he told the woman coldly. "It has been made ready for their use, and, as you know, is large enough to accommodate even his Tlascalan allies."

Again the woman translated the speech to Malinche, who nodded gravely and signaled the squire to help him mount. Without even waiting to make sure that he was followed, Cuitlahua started off on foot. Now that his emperor had gone he walked proudly, with his head held high, and there was something in his manner that told Chimal that Montezuma's brother did not welcome these visitors, nor regard them as gods.

As soon as Cuitlahua was out of earshot Chimal called down to Eecatl.

"The emperor's gone! Come back up."

Others heard his voice, and there was a quick scramble up the rocks.

"I don't see how you got up so soon," admired Eecatl. "Especially Atototl. I wonder what's been happening."

"I imagine they just met and talked," said Atototl innocently.

It took some time for the army to resume its march. Malinche changed his formation, and now instead of riding two abreast there were four riders advancing across the bridge. As before, the people were more interested in the strange animals than in the men.

"Listen to the sound their paws make against the stone," marveled Eecatl. "Their feet are hard, not soft like other animals'."

"Look!" screamed Atototl, forgetting herself and raising her voice. "Here comes Quetzal! It's Quetzal himself!"

There was a murmur among the onlookers. For the

first time the people forgot the animals, for every eye was fastened on a single rider now coming in to view.

He was a big man, on a roan mount. Like the others, he was encased in shining silver, but the sun had beat uncomfortably on his crested helmet, and he had taken it off; he rode with bared head, and the clear light shone on hair as yellow as maize. It was cut off just above his shoulders, but in the front he wore a full beard, which lay in long golden waves across his armored chest.

"Quetzal! Quetzal!" cried Atototl, hoisting herself high on thin arms made strong and muscular from long hours at the loom. "Welcome, Quetzal!"

"Atototl!" reproved Chimal quickly, and all the people turned to stare at the rude girl who had so forgotten her manners.

But the golden-haired man on the red steed heard her and did not seem displeased. The silken beard parted in a smile, and he raised a gauntleted hand in salute as he rode by.

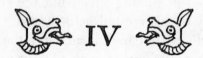 IV

When Chimal and Eecatl reported to Ocelotl the following morning they found the old soldier chipping obsidian for a fresh sword edge.

"There'll be no lesson today." His old voice cracked with importance. "I've no time to bother with children. At any moment I may be called."

"Called for what?" asked Chimal in surprise. It was all he could do to keep from taking the sharp stone from the old man. Ocelotl's hands trembled so with age that he was in danger of cutting himself.

"For war!" The black eyes in the wrinkled face blazed up at them with the vigor of remembered youth before Ocelotl bent his gray head again to his task. "Last night Lord Cuitlahua, he who commands the warriors, sent word to every *telpochcalli*. Speed up the training of our young men, he said. Send word to all experienced warriors to stand ready for instant call. Two thousand of our old enemy have been admitted to the city, and nearly half a hundred white-skinned strangers. It is too early yet to know why they have come, but we must be prepared whenever the emperor gives the word."

"But if it was Quetzal who came yesterday there'll be no war," protested Chimal. "Quetzal is a god of peace and love."

"Who said it was Quetzal?" snapped Ocelotl. "Not my Lord Cuitlahua, else he would not have given that order."

"But we saw him, didn't we, Eecatl?" Chimal insisted stubbornly. "He has the hair and beard of Quetzal. And Montezuma, who knows everything, received him kindly."

"He must be a god of some kind," added Eecatl a little fearfully. "Last night, after his army had gone into the Palace of Axaya', where they are quartered, long black noses appeared above the palace wall—"

"They were hollow tubes," interrupted Chimal. "Made of blackened silver, probably. Don't you remember, we saw them in the line of march yesterday?"

"Anyway," continued Eecatl, "without warning they began to roar, all at once. We heard them clear out here at Tlaltelolco, only I thought it was thunder. People said that they blew out great blasts of smoke that smelled like a volcano, and that the stone wall rocked and shook, and that bricks tumbled from buildings all around."

"So?" Ocelotl seemed startled. He was a little hard of hearing, and so missed much of the gossip. A moment later he recovered himself. "Perhaps there is *some* magic about the strangers. But it is not Quetzal's kind of magic, and our gods are stronger than theirs. We must hold fast to that belief and prepare to defend ourselves when the time comes."

"Then that's all the more reason why we should have our lesson," argued Eecatl, forgetting that only a moment before he had been uneasy about the supernatural powers of the stranger. "You're too old to fight, Ocelotl, but Chimal and I—"

"Who says I am too old?" Ocelotl's voice rose

37

in anger. He reached out and rapped Eecatl's bare ankles with the flat surface of the obsidian stone. "My hand has not lost its cunning with the javelin. Perhaps I cannot run, but I can still fight for Anahuac."

"Of course you can, Ocelotl," soothed Chimal quickly. "Eecatl only meant that we need to learn from your experience now more than ever."

"Then go to the *telpochcalli*," Ocelotl told him sulkily. "It is their job to train young warriors. I have given them your names. They are expecting you."

"Now? You mean today?" cried Eecatl in delight.

"Did you give them my name too?" asked Chimal quickly. Perhaps, if war was imminent he would not be needed as a priest. Perhaps he could go to the *telpochcalli* with his friend, and be a warrior.

"They asked what youths I had been training." Ocelotl tried the honed edge of obsidian against his thumb, and grunted with satisfaction at the thin line of red that sprang up on the skin. "I told them you two. But I told them also that Chimal was pledged to the priesthood and would be going to the *calmecac*. They too have had word from Lord Cuitlahua. The training you will have there now will be for war."

"You see!" Eecatl pounded Chimal's back with excitement. "You don't have to be a priest yet. Maybe you'll be such a good warrior, and you'll lead your men so well, that the priests at the *calmecac* will decide that that's where you should stay."

"It has happened before," agreed Ocelotl encouragingly. "Remember everything I have taught you. Be fearless in battle. You have nothing to lose, and everything to gain."

"I only wish you could be with me." Eecatl looked at Chimal wistfully.

"So he can, for this morning, at least," declared Ocelotl. "Before either of you can report to his school you must visit the barber and have your hair cut in a *piochtli*. Now go. Go. You are distracting me from my work."

There was no question but that Lord Cuitlahua's orders were being carried out. As the boys crossed the grounds of the *telpochcalli* they saw that every training space was occupied. Young men battled each other with swords, and arrows sang through the air as they speeded toward the targets. Those working on arms had no time to waste in idle talk this morning, and the drying racks were lined solid with freshly bent bows.

"Tomorrow," anticipated Eecatl with shining eyes, "no, this afternoon, I'll be one of those out there. Will you enter the *calmecac* today, do you think?"

"I'll have to ask my father. This is market day, so he'll be at the *tianquez*. As soon as I've had my hair cut I'll look for him."

Chimal wondered what Ollin would say when he heard that military training was being rushed ahead. Although he had agreed with Teteoni that his son should fulfill his birth dedication and be a priest, he had not been in any hurry to enter him in the *calmecac*. There was plenty of time for that, he once had declared.

"I wonder when war will start," said Eecatl thoughtfully.

"It can't begin until Montezuma gives the word. Lord Cuitlahua can speed up the training, but no one can start a war but the emperor himself," said Chimal.

Although between forty and fifty thousand people visited the *tianquez* at Tlaltelolco on market day, it was not a noisy place. The uniformed guardians who patrolled the passageways laid out like regular streets on the red polished pavement made sure that business was conducted in a quiet, orderly fashion. Merchandise was arranged according to kind, so that all the foodstuff was in one area, all the wearing apparel in another. At the far end sat a judicial court, perpetually in session, so that anyone caught cheating or pilfering could be instantly charged and tried.

Ordinarily Chimal and Eecatl took their time passing through the market. Everything anyone could dream of was displayed in elaborate stalls, or spread out on woven mats in front of vendors, who sat cross-legged on the paving. There were jewels, turquoise and amethyst, emeralds and pearls, set in bracelets and earrings and nose plugs of gold and silver; feathers of falcons and eagles and sparrow hawks, as well as those from the brilliantly hued tropical birds, the quetzal, the hummingbird, and the parrot. There were skins of puma and deer, foxes and jaguar, tanned or made into rich robes; and cloaks and loincloths and shirts made from cotton or fiber of the aloes. There were rolls of paper made from bark, and stacks of wood; thick knots of pine, dripping pitch, for building fires, builders' wood, reed and bamboo; medicines, poultices, and ointments; shoes and ropes; matting and screens, tables and chests. There were dishes of earthenware and of painted wood, calabashes and vases, flint and obsidian knives, and spoons made of tortoise shell or of silver.

To the boys the produce section was the most fascinating of all, for here were delicacies to set anyone's mouth to watering: maize, beans, peppers, onions, squash, tomatoes, juicy pears, apples and bananas, both yellow and red, and, from the hot countries, the spiny pineapple. The meat stalls sold hares, turkeys, venison, duck, and hairless dogs, and next to them were displayed all the produce of the lake, fish and frogs and crustaceans. As if the sight of these foodstuffs were not enough, there were tantalizing cooking smells as well. In one section women baked maize cakes and tortillas, filled with meat or fruit, over small braziers, and offered them for sale.

Today, however, neither boy had time for looking. It was one of the most important moments in either of their lives: the official cutting of a *piochtli,* the formal haircut that would designate them as having been enrolled in school.

The barbers, with their special section in the market, sat on one end of a mat, their customers on the other. Working with sharp stone knives, they wrought transformations that could be read by all Aztecs. When a barber had finished, a youngster became a schoolboy, an untried warrior was transformed into one who had achieved his first victory, and a warrior was changed into a priest.

"Ah," said the barber as he saw them approaching. "My Lord Cuitlahua has sent me much business today. Sit down. I know what you require without your having to tell me."

"I enter the *telpochcalli* today," announced Eecatl importantly. No barber was going to do him out of the pleasure of saying the words. "And my friend enters the *calmecac.*"

"The *piochtli* is the same for the both," said the barber placidly, beginning on the long hair that grew from the crown of Eecatl's head. "The students of the *telpochcalli* and the *calmecac* may be rivals, and quar-

41

rel a little, but one thing they must share: the same *piochtli*."

He worked swiftly, and in no time at all he had finished and was holding up a small mirror made of polished obsidian, so that his customer might see the result.

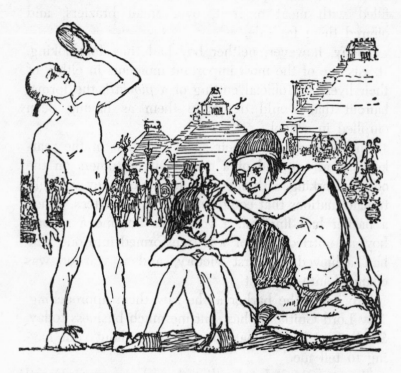

Eecatl stared at his reflection with delight. His hair, which had hung to his shoulders, was now cut short, with the exception of a single long lock left growing on the nape of his neck. This was the official *piochtli*, mark of a beginning student. He must wear it until he had taken his first prisoner in war. Then the tail in back would be cut, and the hair grown to fall over his right ear. This would be called an *iyac*.

42

"How do I look?" he demanded.

"Wonderful," admired Chimal enviously. "Now it's my turn."

It was amazing what a difference the haircut made, thought Chimal. His head felt pounds lighter, and the glimpse he had in the obsidian mirror convinced him that it added years to his age. Why, people would think him at least thirteen in his new *piochtli*, maybe even older!

"Shall we go find your father and show him?" Eecatl tossed his head proudly, reaching around to make sure that the tail lay smoothly in place.

"I guess we'd better," agreed Chimal soberly. For the first time he questioned the wisdom of having a *piochtli* without permission from his parents. Perhaps they would not be so happy about it.

Since his last trading expedition had been to the coast, Ollin's goods had been of an assorted nature, including chocolate and vanilla beans, pineapple, and shell ornaments. They would be displayed in various parts of the market under the supervision of such trusty slaves as Cipactli and Tecpatl, Ollin's most trusted aide and second in command. But the trader himself would be sure to supervise the sale of the most valuable commodity of all, the mosaic featherwork, and Chimal led the way to the area reserved for this most intricate form of art.

Eecatl followed slowly. He paused to look into every passing face in the hope that someone would notice his new haircut, and he fell so far behind that Chimal had to stop and wait for him.

"Come on," he said. "I want to get this over with."

"Over with?" Eecatl seemed surprised; then his face

brightened. "Oh, I see. You mean so we can enroll in school. I'd almost forgotten. Come on, then."

This time it was Eecatl who hurried ahead and who found the booth of the *pochteca* first. Ollin was on his feet, speaking with a customer whose back was turned, but who must have been very rich, for she wore many golden bracelets on her arms and her over-blouse was heavy with embroidery.

To interrupt a good sale was the worst mistake any-one could make, and Chimal tried to call Eecatl back, but Eecatl did not hear. He took up a stand just behind the customer, tossing his head proudly and waiting to be noticed. Chimal stepped forward to pull his friend away, but it was too late. Ollin had looked over the lady's shoulder and seen his son. His mouth dropped open in sur-prise.

"Chimal!"

"Yes, sir. We'll be back later, when you're not busy." He apologized hastily, tugging on Eecatl's arm, but Ollin stepped around the customer and grasped Chimal's shoulders.

"Chimal! What have you done?"

"Ocelotl told us to get *piochtlis*," explained Eecatl. "He says Lord Cuitlahua has ordered all the warriors to stand ready, and the training to be speeded up in the schools. Ocelotl says that he can teach us no more, and that we are to enter the *telpochcalli* and the *calmecac* right away."

"My Lord Cuitlahua is taking a great deal on him-self," said a soft voice beside them, and Chimal saw that the customer had turned around. He glanced at her briefly, then looked again, this time more carefully. He had seen her before. She was the Aztec woman who had arrived with the white-skinned strangers, the

44

one who had acted as interpreter for Montezuma and Malinche.

"There will be no war." She smiled at them each in turn, and Chimal could not help noticing how pretty she was. "Montezuma will not call for war. He knows that the strangers come in peace." She looked inquiringly at Ollin. "Are these your sons?"

"This is my son, Chimalpopoca." Ollin's voice sounded strange and a little troubled. "This is his friend Eecatl. And this is the lady Malinche, whom I met many years ago."

"No, no, Ollin," she protested quickly. "That name is no longer mine. I gave it to my lord, the leader of the white-skinned soldiers. By his own people he is called Hernán Cortés, but that name comes hard to our Aztec tongues, so it pleases him to use mine. In exchange he has given me a new name. I am Doña Marina."

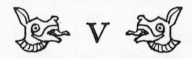

V

It was a full week before Chimal entered the *calmecac* in Tenochtitlán. Now that he had relinquished publicly his boyhood by having his hair cut in a *piochtli* there was no turning back, but his mother and father kept him at home as long as they dared.

"Once you have gone you can never return to us." Mazatl sighed wistfully. "Except for short visits."

"If you had only dedicated me to the warriors instead of to the priesthood it would be different," Chimal could not help pointing out. "Then, after three years' service, I could always come home. I could have been a trader like you, Father."

"Perhaps we were wrong," admitted Ollin. "But you are very dear to us, my son. The body of a priest is sacred."

"Oh, yes," Mazatl agreed fervently. "Warriors run great dangers. If they are taken in battle nothing can save them from the sacrifice. And traders too live perilous lives. Every time your father leaves us on one of his long expeditions I worry until he returns. Do you think the mourning that a trader's family wears while he is away means nothing? We have been fortunate, Chimal. Yacatecuhtli has had your father in his special care."

"I'm not afraid," insisted Chimal stubbornly. "And

46

I'd rather run the danger of being killed myself than taking another's life."

"Making a sacrifice to the gods is not killing," defended Mazatl quickly. She came from a family that had given many members to the priesthood, and she was well trained in its traditions. "Man was created by the sacrifice of the gods. Now he must reciprocate in blood. Without the daily sacrifice to Tonatiuh the sun would not travel across the sky. We would have no crops. The rain would never fall without sacrifice to Tlaloc, and our rivers and lakes dry up. In the end we would all perish."

"Quetzal didn't believe in sacrifice."

"But Quetzal went away. He fled to escape the vengeance of the other gods who did believe in it," Chimal's mother reminded him. "Now we must serve those gods. You especially, since you have been dedicated to them."

"Maybe that's why Quetzal came back with an army," suggested Chimal thoughtfully. "Maybe he isn't planning to fight us, but the other gods."

"Quetzal hasn't returned," said Ollin with a frown. "Those strangers are not gods but men. Lord Cuitlahua is wiser than his brother Montezuma in this matter."

"Hush," warned Mazatl in alarm. "You must not speak so. Montezuma is the emperor, and his will must be ours."

On the appointed day Ollin took his son to the temple school in Tenochtitlán. They went in one of the larger canoes, paddled by Cipactli and Tecpatl. Tecpatl seldom wielded a paddle any more. Years ago he had lost an arm in battle, and his position as Ollin's

47

chief aide made such menial tasks unnecessary. That he asked to be allowed to do so today was the mark of his affection for Chimal. As for Cipactli, he wept openly all the way.

"It will never be the same," he complained. "The old days are gone. When you come to visit us again you will be wearing a long black, evil-smelling robe, and you will be thin from fasting."

"I won't be wearing a robe for years," Chimal pointed out. Cipactli was making him feel worse. "They won't even let me wear a *tilmatli*, nothing but a loincloth."

"And your hair will be matted, and your young skin scarred with thorns," wailed Cipactli. "And tomorrow we lose the little Atototl too, when she enters the *ichpochtlaque*, the school for young girls."

"She's lucky." Chimal scowled enviously. "She gets to go to the school in Tlaltelolco. She doesn't have to go all the way to Tenochtitlán the way I do."

When they neared the temple square Ollin told the boatmen to bring the canoe to shore so that they might finish the journey on foot. Perhaps he was tired of Cipactli's tears, or possibly he wanted these last few moments alone with his son.

Father and son stepped out on the broad causeway that extended from Tlacopan to the western precincts of the temple. Beside them ran the high walls enclosing the Palace of Axaya'. Chimal immediately looked up, his eyes seeking the metal tubes that could speak with voices of thunder, and belch black, sulfurous smoke. There they were, dark against the blue sky, pointing toward the Great Pyramid, which towered above the smaller Temple of the Sun across the way.

The street was unusually crowded this afternoon, and it became even more so as they walked along. What was even stranger, many of the throng were nobles, who customarily spent this hour after dinner in a siesta, and dark-robed priests, who seldom ventured outside the temple square. No one seemed to be going anywhere. They stood patiently in the street, their faces solemn and a little frightened, as though they were waiting for something to happen.

"What is it, Father?" asked Chimal.

"I don't know." Ollin's eyes were wary, and his face grew taut. He reached out to grasp his son's arm, and together they pushed through the center pathway courteously left open by the crowd.

As they reached the palace gates Chimal caught the flash of sunlight on the armor of the guards who stood firmly, barring the great wooden doors. Then, suddenly, the silent crowd began to murmur. It was as though a whisper was being passed along from one to another, and the news must have been bad, for the apprehension on each man's face was changed to anger.

The center pathway widened as the people fell back on either side, and Chimal's ears caught a clanking noise that he had heard before. It was the silver armor of the white-skinned strangers, and it was approaching through the crowd. Chimal had not been in Tenochtitlán since their arrival, and he wondered if crowds still turned out to watch the visitors march by. Then he saw that on either side of him people were falling to their knees, and he felt Ollin jerk his arm as a signal that he should do the same.

It was not as easy to observe the strangers today as it had been on the bridge, but by tilting his downcast head Chimal was able to get a partial view. First came a troop of armed soldiers, their lances drawn to hold back anyone who might venture from the sidelines. They were followed by four men in armor, with their swords in their hands, their visors closed, and after that came the emperor himself. Montezuma rode in his golden litter, carried by four nobles, and his face looked drawn with misery. Behind him walked a great number of his court, some of whom made no attempt to hide the tears that ran down their cheeks. Another company of armed soldiers brought up the rear, and as soon as they had passed, the people stood up, filling the path.

"What does it mean, Father?" Chimal demanded. Now there was no need to keep his voice low, for the people were crying out in anger.

"I don't know," said Ollin. "Listen!"

Above the protests of the crowd rose the sound of the royal conch shell. It was a call for silence, and obediently the people ceased their angry mutterings. A second later they heard the voice of the emperor speaking to them from just outside the palace gate.

"Do not be alarmed, my children. Continue on about your business. I go to stay a while with my friends, who are called Spaniards, and who come to us from across the sea. I go of my own free will, and as proof of my love for them."

The protests were not resumed after Montezuma stopped speaking, but people looked at each other with astonishment. The emperor was the emperor, and his decision could not be questioned. But what did it mean? Why was he leaving his own great palace to stay with the strangers? What could he possibly accomplish? And to what could it lead? They dispersed slowly, shaking their heads.

"I wish you had not rushed things by having that

piochtli," murmured Ollin as they moved on. "You are so young, and I would feel safer having you under my own roof."

Chimal had been inside the temple enclosure of Tenochtitlán before, but today he seemed to see everything with new eyes. From now on, this was to be his home, and he felt overwhelmed.

It was a great, flat area, a hundred and seventy-five by five hundred yards, bounded on the north by the Pyramid of the Sun, on the south by a canal, on the east by the two-story residence of high dignitaries, and on the west by the front of Montezuma's palace. The double pyramid of Huitzil and Tlaloc, gods of war and of growing things, towered above all the others. It was a hundred and fifty feet high, and the two temples, one painted red, the other blue, that crowned the peak, were reached by three flights of three hundred and sixty steps, which wound around the sloping sides from base to summit. A great stone wall decorated with carved snakes' heads encircled the Great Pyramid, and each of the four gates was guarded day and night by a young priest.

Scattered about the square were over twenty-five lesser pyramids, and while some were larger than others, they all looked the same, with the exception of Quetzal's temple. That was round, a pleasing shape to the god of winds and men, and the doorway was carved to represent the open jaws of a plumed serpent. Each pyramid-temple had its own grainery and store-house, as well as its own *calmecac* and priests' houses. A separate building housed the school for the religious musicians, and in addition there were several arsenals, many fasting houses, five oratories, two ball courts, two root cellars, a dancing place, many carved stones

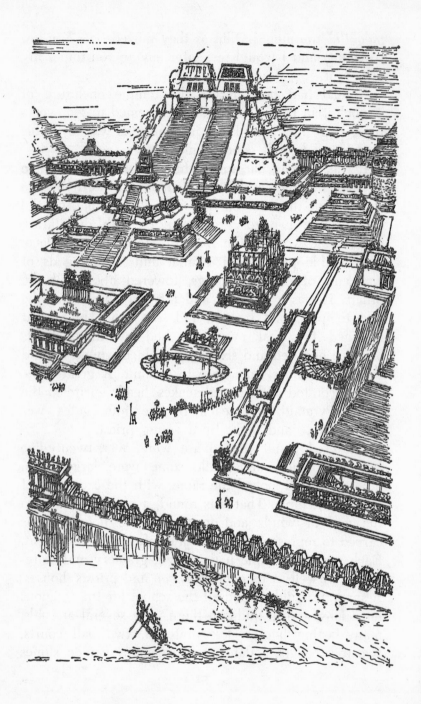

of religious significance, and seven skull racks, on which the bleached mementos of the constant sacrifices to the gods were stacked. The temple square had its own wells for drinking water, three bathing places, and a star column, from which astrologers could study the movements in the heavens. In spite of all these buildings, there still remained ample space for worshipers to gather at celebrations. It had never looked so huge and terrifying as it did today, nor made Chimal feel quite so small.

Ollin looked down at his son and smiled encouragingly.

"You will learn your way around," he said. "It will not always be so strange. We go this way. First is the Temple of Coacalo. Next to it is *your* temple, the Temple of Coatlique."

Like the others, Coatlique's pyramid rose in terraces from a wide base. The goddess whom Chimal was to serve was the mother of the sun, moon, and stars, and because she was known as the Lady of the Skirt of Serpents, carved heads of snakes decorated the railings on either side of the stairway leading to the top. Both Ollin and Chimal were careful not to touch the carvings as they climbed.

The heavy scent of burning copal, which hung over the whole enclosure, grew stronger as they mounted, and Chimal's eyes began to smart. No wonder his Uncle Teteoni's eyes were always bloodshot, he thought. Before long the same thing would happen to him.

As they started up the third flight a boy only a little older than Chimal came hurrying down to intercept them. He wore a loincloth of roughly woven cotton, and there were swollen red scratches on his thin arms and legs.

"Your coming has been observed by the high priest," he told them civilly. "He has sent me to ask your name, and what you seek of the goddess."

"I am Ollin, the *pochteca*. And this is my son, Chimal-popoca, who has come to redeem his birth pledge."

"Oh," said the boy. He looked at Chimal, and his brown eyes lightened with friendship. "I will tell Teteoni. Wait here. I will ask when he will talk with you."

"Don't you think Uncle Teteoni recognized us?" whispered Chimal when the boy had gone.

"Maybe not," said Ollin dryly. "Or maybe he's just reminding us that he is the high priest and that we must await his pleasure."

In a few minutes the boy returned. He seemed impressed with the reception about to be accorded them.

"Teteoni bids me bring you both to the temple," he told them. Then he added confidentially, "That's very unusual. Generally strangers have to wait below until Teteoni is willing to see them. I've know them to wait for as long as three days."

"Teteoni is my mother's brother," explained Chimal. "She'd be very cross if my father didn't get home before then."

The boy seemed to find this very strange. Perhaps he had never thought of the high priest as a member of someone's family.

As they mounted the last flight another odor began mingling with the incense, an unpleasant scent that made Chimal wrinkle his nose. It was like Uncle Teteoni's robes, he realized. His eyes were really burning now, and he wondered again how he could ever stand to be a priest.

The stairs ended in a flat area on which was erected a tower-like apartment open on one side to the square below. This was the temple. It was built of wood, lightly covered with thin plaster that served as a foundation for gold and flashing jewel adornments. Banners of bright featherwork mosaic fluttered gently on either side. Their guide must have sensed the awe that filled them both, for he smiled encouragingly as he led them on to the open doorway.

Within were a heavy stone of polished jaspar, raised at one end and as long as the body of a man, a huge cylindrical drum made of serpent's skin, conch shells for sounding the hours after dark, and many smoke-blackened baskets filled with knives. Incense curled from an altar before a huge, jewel-bedecked statue of the goddess, and as they arrived a priest threw a handful of fresh copal on the fire, causing it to flare with blue and scarlet flames.

Then Teteoni came from behind the carved figure to greet them.

"I am glad you are here," he said. "Every day the signs grow worse. I have been worried about the safety of my nephew. I want him under the protection of our Lady of the Skirt of Serpents. Let her look at you, Chimalpopoca, so she will know you for her own."

He pushed the boy forward, and Chimal was forced to look up at the great carved figure. Although she was the mother goddess, there was nothing about Coatlique to inspire love. Her feet were clawed, and her arms terminated in snake heads. Her skirt was a mass of braided rattlesnakes, while around her neck and hanging over her breast was a necklace of carved hands and hearts. The head of the carving was the same front and back, and was formed of two serpents meeting face to face.

"Why do you say the signs grow worse, Teteoni?" asked Ollin guardedly.

"I was wrong. The strangers who have come are not from Quetzal," declared Teteoni darkly. "They worship another god, and they do not honor ours. They are wicked, greedy men. They have broken into the sealed treasure house of the gods, and now even the least of them wears golden chains and jeweled bracelets that rightfully belong to the temple."

"Perhaps it was with Montezuma's permission." Ollin's voice was expressionless, but his eyes narrowed with anger. "Just now, as we came along the street, his litter passed us on the way to the Palace of Axaya'. He called to the people that he was going there to live with his friends."

"Do you speak the truth?" Teteoni's scarred face grew pale, and his thin shoulders trembled under his black robe. He gathered up his long skirts and started down the steps, calling over his shoulder to the boy who had escorted them to the temple. "Quauhtli, I leave my nephew in your charge! Take him to the *calmecac*."

"Your news is upsetting to our high priest." Quauhtli's voice was apologetic, but his eyes danced at the task that had been assigned him. "Doubtless he hurries to share it with those in the Great Temple."

"He may find that they already know. There were priests in the crowd as the emperor went by," Ollin recalled.

Led by Quauhtli, they descended the three flights of stairs to the square below. Now that he was no longer in the awesome presence of the high priest their guide chattered eagerly, answering Chimal's questions. He was almost thirteen, he told them, and in his second year at the *calmecac*. He was the son of a noble from a distant province, and was destined not for the priesthood but as a leader of warriors. He could hardly wait for an opportunity to prove his bravery in battle.

"But will they send you so soon?" asked Chimal.

"Probably not yet." Quauhtli shrugged his thin, bare shoulders ruefully. "But this year I'm to be permitted to take part in the religious dances to Huitzil. And that's the first step."

Chimal wanted to walk to the outer gate with his father, and Quauhtli eagerly agreed. Once they reported to the *calmecac* they would both be put to work, he told them. Students had no time for wandering around the temple grounds. And there were long periods of enforced silence too, which might account for the great flow of words coming from him now. Chimal had never met a boy with so much to say.

Quauhtli was trotting a little ahead, speaking over his shoulder to Chimal and his father, when suddenly he stopped short.

"Look!" They had just rounded the corner of the Great Pyramid, and the finger that he pointed trembled with excitement. "Men dressed in shining silver. Are those some of the strangers they call Spaniards?"

Several figures were descending the last flight of stairs from the temple. One was a woman, the others were soldiers in full armor. At the base of the pyramid, waiting to receive them, was a small knot of priests.

"Yes," agreed Chimal absently. His own eyes were on the woman. It was the one who called herself Doña Marina. He had tried to ask his father more about her, but Ollin had been noncommittal. She was just someone he had met on his travels years ago, he said. He had almost forgotten her, but she remembered him, and had come up to speak to him in the market. He had no idea how she came to be with the strangers.

"I've never seen one of them," declared Quauhtli. "I've been afraid they'd be driven from the city before I had a chance."

"Didn't you watch them march in?" asked Chimal in surprise. "The palace where they're quartered is just across the way. You could have had the best view of all."

Quauhtli wrinkled his nose.

"You've a lot to learn about being a student. We spent the whole day in prayer and fasting. Come on, let's get up close."

"I wouldn't go too close," warned Ollin, smiling. "I'm afraid one of those priests waiting at the bottom is Teteoni."

Quauhtli hesitated only a second.

"It's worth the penance I'll have to make for wasting time," he decided, and rushed ahead.

Chimal and Ollin followed more slowly, pausing just short of the black-robed men who waited silently for the strangers to leave their most sacred shrine. The soldiers' armor clanked and banged noisily as they came down the stairs. Their visors were raised, and from the openings their eyes, blue, gray, and brown, exchanged insolent glances with the silent priests at the bottom. Doña Marina came last; she held up her long skirt with one jeweled hand, picking her way carefully and pretending not to notice the disapproving glares of her countrymen. Just as she reached the bottom she glanced over and saw the three behind the priests. Her face brightened with a smile.

"Why, it's Ollin, the *pochteca!*" she cried warmly. With her shining head held high she swept past the scowling priests. "What are you doing here? Why aren't you in Tlaltelolco at the market?"

"Today my son enters the *calmecac,* Malinche," answered Ollin. His tone was gruff, and Chimal looked at his father in surprise. Ollin had always observed the greatest courtesy. His son had never heard him speak so abruptly.

"Doña Marina," she corrected smiling, but her cheeks glowed pink, and Chimal thought that she too must have noticed the lack of manners. "It must grieve you to part with him so soon. And it will not be easy for him either, to be away from home for the first time."

Ollin nodded gravely, but did not reply. After a moment Doña Marina turned and spoke directly to Chimal.

"If you get homesick for your mother sometime, come and see me," she invited. "I am just across the way, in the Palace of Axaya'. Perhaps it will help to get away from all the dark robes and incense for an hour or two. The guards will let you pass if you ask for Doña Marina. Tell them you are a friend of mine."

Without waiting for an answer, she smiled and hurried after the soldiers who had continued on across the square.

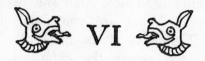

VI

"The priests are upset," confided Quauhtli softly. He spoke from a corner of his mouth, and the only movement of his lips seemed to come from the rhythmic chewing of the maize cake that comprised their midday meal. "I've never seen them so worked up. Something is going on."

Chimal raised his eyebrows, mutely asking for more details. In the past week he had not yet mastered the other students' skill in speaking while avoiding detection by the priests during the periods of enforced silence. It was something he intended to learn. If he didn't he'd be left out of everything, and there was far more to attending the *calmecac* than study and fasting and penance. Although Chimal didn't know how the carefully supervised students managed to uncover their information, they missed little of the gossip and intrigue within the temple or in the world outside.

"I think it has to do with the Spaniards," confided Quauhtli, chewing busily.

Of course it would have, thought Chimal. All news these days had to do with the strangers quartered in the Palace of Axaya'. Only a few days ago the Spaniards had carried out a public execution, and although no student of the *calmecac* was present, each one knew more about it than most of the witnesses.

A small settlement of Spaniards had been left at the coast, and a tribal chief named Quauhpopoca had attacked the fort. In the battle one Spaniard and one of their magic beasts, which the students said were called "horses," had been killed. As soon as the news reached the capital Montezuma had sent for Quauhpopoca and his officers, and on their arrival they were seized and burned to death by the Spaniards as a warning that no Aztec must take arms against them. The execution had taken place in the great market, where everyone could see, and the fire had been made of arrows, javelins, and other weapons taken, by the emperor's order, from the temple arsenals.

The people had watched in amazement, wondering at this strange punishment devised by their ruler, but the students at the *calmecac* agreed that it was not by Montezuma's orders, but should be blamed on Malinche.

"Why doesn't the emperor do something?" puzzled Chimal, when he first heard the story. "He's the only one who can call out the army, and if he'd only say the word a hundred thousand fighting men would answer."

"In the beginning he thought that the strangers might be Quetzal and his followers," explained Quauhtli. His face had grown solemn with remembrance. "You'll never believe the presents Montezuma sent when he first heard that their water-houses had landed on the coast. One day I had permission to leave the temple square, and I saw the caravan set out. There were a hundred porters, and the gold and jewels and feather-work they carried would have filled Coatlique's shrine to overflowing. Montezuma tried to stop the strangers from coming. He forbade them to come, and sent even more treasure, hoping to buy them off, but they wouldn't be stopped. It was as though the presents only made them greedier for more. Then, when they arrived, and Montezuma realized that they were men, not gods, they made him prisoner."

"I myself heard him say that he was their guest," protested Chimal, but his tone was uncertain. Sometimes he wondered if he had actually heard the emperor right.

"He had to say that. They told him to," said Quauhtli with a scowl. "Oh, if Cuitlahua were only emperor, or Cacama, or Guatemozin! They're strong men! Warriors! How different things would be."

"Montezuma was a warrior once," remembered Chimal.

"Once." Quauhtli's tone had been significant.

Today, as soon as they had finished eating, the students of Coatlique's *calmecac* trooped outside. This was one of two hours in the twenty-four during which they were free to do as they pleased. All other time was occupied with assigned duties and sleep.

"Whatever is going on has something to do with the Great Pyramid," observed one of the boys thoughtfully. "I was sent on an errand this morning, and every priest of both Huitzil and Tlaloc must have been gathered on top. There were so many black robes, I could hardly see the shrines."

"Maybe it has something to do with the new month," suggested Chimal shyly. "The great feast of Huitzil will be upon us soon."

"No. I have seen preparations for such feasts before." The boy, one of the older students, spoke in a superior tone of voice, and Chimal wished that he had kept silent. "I would know if that's all it meant."

"If we walk out on the square maybe we can see what they're doing," said Quauhtli quickly.

They had hardly started away from their own temple when the voice of one of the younger priests, calling from the doorway, brought them to a standstill.

"Young men!"

"What is this?" muttered Quauhtli out of the corner of his mouth. "Some special penance that takes away our free hour?"

"Is Chimalpopoca among you?" called the priest.

"What did you do that you shouldn't, Chimal?" whispered someone.

His cheeks flaming, Chimal stepped forward. He could think of no reason why he should be singled out.

"The high priest wishes to see you," said the young priest coldly. "He awaits you in his dining hall."

"Teteoni will know what's going on. See if you can pump him," whispered Quauhtli as Chimal obediently started back to the *calmecac.*

The dining hall for the priests, like the other rooms in the *calmecac,* was bare of furniture. Teteoni was the only occupant. He sat cross-legged on a pile of mats, and Chimal, who had scarcely seen his uncle since he entered the school, was astonished at the change that had come over him.

The high priest had aged in the single week. His skin sagged loosely over the bones, and the scars on his face were almost lost in the many new wrinkles. He was sipping from a cup of water, for this was one of the many fast days when solid food was not permitted him. He seemed unaware that his nephew had entered the room, and even when Chimal crossed over and stood directly before him, his eyes remained clouded and unseeing.

Bending respectfully, Chimal carried his hand from the floor to his head and cleared his throat. When Teteoni did not acknowledge the salute he ventured to speak.

"You sent for me, honored sir?"

Teteoni came to with a visible start.

"Chimalpopoca," he said vaguely. "Yes, Chimalpopoca. Perhaps you can be of service to us. Perhaps the gods have singled you out."

Chimal felt himself grow cold. What could Teteoni possibly mean? Certainly not that he had been chosen as a sacrifice! He wanted to turn and run away, but his legs had grown heavy and he could not lift them.

"Sit down, Chimal," said Teteoni kindly, motioning to a mat opposite him. It seemed to the trembling boy that there was a strange, wild light in those black eyes now focusing upon himself. "I see that I will have to take you into our confidence."

Chimal sank weakly to the floor, moistening his dry lips with his tongue.

"You know about the men called Spaniards," began Teteoni, "those greedy, evil men. You know some of the wicked things they have done: stolen treasure from the gods, taken our emperor and bewitched him so that he no longer knows what he is doing."

Chimal nodded without speaking.

"They make mockery of our gods," continued Teteoni bitterly. "They have tried to forbid the daily sacrifice, and so bring an end to the world. Montezuma knows better than to permit that. But he has agreed to something that is such an insult to the gods of Anahuac that I cannot answer for the consequences."

"Yes?" gasped Chimal weakly. His uncle had paused, and he knew that he was expected to say something.

65

"He has said that the Spaniards may make a place for their god in one of the two temples atop the Great Pyramid!" Teteoni's words were sharp with venom; his eyes blazed with hatred. "This day Tlaloc was removed from his own shrine and forced to share the same one with Huitzil."

For a moment Chimal forgot that Teteoni had suggested that he himself had a special role in this terrible event. Instead he remembered Quauhtli's parting orders to discover anything he could about what was going on. Now he knew all of it! What news he would have to tell the other students later on!

"Huitzil and Tlaloc will be avenged of this insult," added Teteoni darkly. "Rest assured of that. But we must help bring this about if we are to retain their favor. That is where you can help us."

So I am to be a sacrifice, thought Chimal wildly. But why me?

"The other day when you were saying good-by to your father," continued Teteoni, "I saw you greeted by the woman called Marina. I heard her ask you to come and visit her at the Palace of Axaya'."

Chimal stared so blankly that Teteoni frowned and repeated his last sentence.

"Yes," mumbled Chimal miserably.

"I want you to go," ordered Teteoni. "You will call on the lady this afternoon, and when she asks you to come again you will return tomorrow, and the next day, and the next."

Chimal's heart skipped a beat. At least the sacrifice was to be delayed.

"What if she doesn't ask me to come again?" he murmured anxiously.

"You will make yourself so agreeable that she will

want to see you again," commanded Teteoni sternly. "And you will make friends with anyone else in the palace whom you chance to meet."

"Not the Spaniards?"

"Especially the Spaniards," Teteoni said with a nod. "You will observe and remember everything you see and hear."

"But I cannot understand their language."

"Then learn it." The high priest frowned. "And each evening when you return you will report to me everything that you have found out. Everything! We must know what is going on, even before it happens."

"Then I'm not going to be sacrificed after all!" cried Chimal happily. He felt warm, and good all over.

"Sacrificed?" snapped Teteoni. "You have done nothing to merit such an honor. But because the woman Marina has smiled on you, perhaps you can serve the gods by acting as a spy."

VII

"Why, it's Chimal!" Doña Marina put down her embroidery and rose gracefully to her feet. "Did you come to see me?"

"I was homesick," explained Chimal, hoping that his voice would sound convincing. "And I had a few spare hours this afternoon. My lady said that whenever I missed my mother I could visit her."

"The boy is my guest. He is here at my invitation." Marina frowned at the Tlascalan guard who had jerked Chimal roughly up the steps to the terraced rooftop of the palace. "Look at him closely. Memorize his face. Whenever he asks at the gate for me he is to be admitted without question."

Reluctantly the Tlascalan relinquished his grip on Chimal's arm. His fingers left livid marks on the brown skin, but he did not dare dispute the woman's authority. He turned and stalked back down the steps.

"Come sit here beside me, Chimal." Marina smiled and motioned to the piles of mats stacked in the shade of one of many flowering shrubs. "I am glad you could come. I know what it is to be lonely."

Chimal sat down, reminding himself that he was a spy. He had been sent to uncover information, but now that he was here he did not know how to go about it. When he had said "Doña Marina," slowly and carefully, the guards had opened the gate and thrust him into the hands of a vicious Tlascalan, repeating the same words. He in turn had dragged the boy through the vast courtyard and up the stairs so speedily that there had been no chance to observe anything.

"Perhaps you are hungry," suggested Marina gently. She turned and called to a group of serving women who were seated a short distance away. "We will have chocolate."

Chocolate! For a moment Chimal forgot that he was a spy, and his eyes brightened with anticipation. Chocolate was a drink for special occasions. Although it was said that the emperor drank it every day, it came from the hot countries, and even Ollin, a trader, considered it too costly for daily consumption.

The chocolate arrived served in tiny cups made of painted wood, ornamented with gold. It had been mixed with honey and vanilla and beaten to a froth. Chimal had never tasted anything so delicious. He felt like a king, or at least like an important noble, and the thought gave him the confidence to ask a question that had puzzled him many times.

"When did you know my father, Doña Marina?"

"He has never told you?" She seemed surprised. "It was many years ago. My own father was a rich and a powerful chief in the province of Coatzacualco. He died when I was very young and my mother married again, this time to a man who did not possess as great a fortune as my own father. They had a son, and because my mother wanted to give him my father's heritage, which should have gone to me, she told everyone I had died, and secretly gave me as a slave to some traders."

"Not to my father? He would not be a party to such a thing!" Chimal gasped in horror.

"No." Marina shook her head quickly. "These were traders from Xicallanco. But their party fell in with that of Ollin on the way. We traveled together to Tobasco, on the sea coast. Your father was very kind to me. I was frightened and homesick. I can remember how he used to talk to me and try to comfort me. He was the only one in all that company who seemed to care about the tears of a little girl."

"I wish he had bought you and brought you home," said Chimal. "Then you could have been my sister."

"I wished so too at the time." Marina smiled. "But the price asked for me was very high. I was a pretty little girl. They said I showed great promise. But the Tobascan chief who bought me was known to your father. Ollin told me he would be kind to me, and he was."

"Did you ever see my father again?" asked Chimal. He had completely forgotten that he was supposed to be a spy for Teteoni.

"Not until I came here with the Spaniards." Marina sighed a little, without seeming to realize it. "I was given to them by my master, along with nineteen other slaves. That was after the Spaniards conquered the Tobascans. I came with them here, and I recognized your father in the market the moment I saw him. I was overjoyed on seeing him, but he was not so glad to see me."

"It's because—well, some people don't think the Spaniards should have come here." Chimal felt his cheeks burning. He didn't want to hurt Marina. Her life had been sad enough. "They want them to go away."

"They will," she promised quickly. "They only came

to tell our people about the True God. Malinche says that the Aztec gods are things of evil and must be destroyed. The Spaniards will be here only as long as it takes to do that, and to build new ships to take them home."

Chimal started nervously. Such words must surely draw down the wrath of every god of Anahuac. He was amazed that Marina was allowed to sit there unharmed after uttering such blasphemy.

"What are ships?" he asked, when it was evident that the gods intended to withhold their punishment.

"Giant boats—the water-houses that brought the Spaniards across the ocean to our land. Some of the men wished to return home after they had been here a little while, but Malinche wanted to finish his mission. To make sure that everyone remained, and that some of the soldiers did not steal away, he had all the ships but one destroyed."

"Can they build more of these water-houses?"

"Oh, yes." Marina smiled loyally. "Malinche and the other Spaniards can do anything."

With pleased satisfaction Chimal realized that he had uncovered news of value to report to Teteoni when he returned. He set his chocolate cup on the floor, hoping that Marina would notice that it was empty.

"How did you learn to speak the language of the Spaniards?"

"A little at a time. At first I could not understand a word. But I listened carefully, and pointed to this and to that. When I was told the names of things, I remembered. It is not as hard as you might think."

"Could I learn?" asked Chimal cautiously, hoping that he was not going too fast. To his delight, Marina smiled and clapped her hands.

71

"Of course you could." She stood up and beckoned him to rise also. "You're the first Aztec who has wanted to learn. Malinche will be pleased. Come with me. I'm going to take you to the man who helped me most."

"To Malinche?" Chimal caught his breath. Sometime, if he continued coming here, he would have to meet this leader of the Spaniards, but today he was afraid. Things were moving too fast.

"No, no." Marina smiled. "Malinche is too busy to give language lessons to a small boy. I'm taking you to Father Olmedo."

This time there was opportunity to see everything when they went down the stairs. Sentries paced the top of the thick stone walls surrounding the palace grounds, and one of the long metal tubes protruded above each entrance and at every corner. Chimal plucked at Marina's sleeve, pointing.

"Those are the things that belch smoke and sound like thunder. What are they called?"

"Cannon," she told him promptly. "And the arms carried by the sentries along the wall and at the gates are called harquebuses. You see, you have started your lessons in Spanish already."

Chimal's gaze dropped to the courtyard. It was crowded with Tlascalans, over two thousand in all, and since there was no room to house such numbers within the palace itself, they had thrown up rough shelters in the open. Their cooking fires were built on the polished marble of the court, and even though they were not momentarily engaged in combat, they were prepared for instant call. The leaders wore feathered mail, and the common soldiers had painted their bare bodies in corresponding colors. They wore headpieces shaped like animal heads, and their weapons were laid out, close at

72

hand. Chimal had heard that they were experienced warriors. Their archers were said to be able to discharge two or three arrows at a time; no one excelled them in the throwing of javelins; and the slightest blow from one of their two-headed staffs was enough to fell a strong man instantly. Chimal writhed inwardly to see them making themselves so much at home in one of the proudest palaces in Tenochtitlán.

"Don't you hate being friends with the Tlascalans?" he asked impulsively.

Doña Marina smiled gently. "Father Olmedo's chapel is this way," she said, ignoring his question.

Father Olmedo was in one of the ground-floor apartments of the palace, and as he came forward to greet them Chimal remembered having seen him the day the Spaniards crossed the causeway. He had been one of two riders whose mounts were clearly inferior to those who led the force. Their fur was roughly brown and unkempt, and they were so small that the feet of the riders scarcely cleared the ground. They had long ears, and neither of them wore a metallic blanket or silver ornaments. The men who rode them wore long, dark robes, and their heads were bare and partly shaved. One was a thin, sour-faced individual who carried two strips of wood joined together in the form of a cross. He looked straight ahead without glancing at either side, but the other man kept smiling at all those heads staring up at him from the side of the causeway. Occasionally he waved and called out something in a tongue that no one could understand. Father Olmedo was the smiling man.

Marina spoke with him in the strange tongue that Chimal was certain he would never understand,

and the priest nodded happily. He put his hand on the boy's head and smiled down at him.

"He will be glad to help you," said Marina. "First you must learn his name. Father Olmedo. Say it."

Chimal repeated the syllables, and the sounds were strange in his ears.

The priest turned and pointed to a carved figure of a woman hanging above a high table draped with an embroidered cloth.

"Blessed Virgin," he said slowly, and Chimal dutifully imitated the sounds.

"She is the mother of the True God," explained Marina swiftly. "Because Father Olmedo is a priest he will teach you religious words first. But soon you will get on to things of everyday living. Over there"—she pointed to the table—"is the Spaniards' altar. You see how different it is from those of our gods. There is no sacrificial stone. The True God does not believe in human sacrifice."

"Perhaps he is Quetzal?" asked Chimal hopefully.

Marina shook her head.

"No, not Quetzal. There is no Quetzal."

Chimal shivered as he had done on the rooftop when he first heard Marina speak against the gods. Then he began to moan softly. This time, he thought, she has gone too far! For through the open doorway strode a tall figure. Hair the color of gold fell to his shoulders, and a bright beard waved across the silver metal of his breastplate.

Marina bowed deeply. Father Olmedo spoke, and the bright-haired stranger answered them, while Chimal slowly recovered his composure.

Of course it wasn't Quetzal, he reminded himself. It was the Spaniard he had seen that day on the causeway, the one who had smiled and waved at Atototl. Since then the Aztecs had given this man the name of Tonatiuh, after their sun god, because of his golden hair. Chimal had known he was here. He had expected to see him sometime. It was just having the Spaniard appear so suddenly after Marina's blasphemous words that had given him such a start.

While the three were talking he studied the newcomer more carefully. With his hair and beard and bright blue eyes he certainly answered the description of Quetzal. But looking closely, Chimal decided that this stranger could never be the god who loved men. There was something cruel about his face, and much arrogance about his person.

The conversation came to an end, and Marina turned to Chimal.

"There can be no lesson today," she explained. "Father Olmedo has duties at the Great Pyramid, and I too must go. There may be need for an interpreter. Don Pedro has brought word that one of the temples has been made ready for the True God. Mass will be said there this evening."

Chimal nodded. The priests had known this would happen. It was not necessary to warn them. He hoped the other small things he had discovered would prove useful.

"Before you go you must meet Don Pedro Alvarado," remembered Marina. "He is one of Malinche's most trusted lieutenants." She said something in Spanish, and the big blond man looked at Chimal briefly. "You will see much of Don Pedro when you are here at the palace, having your Spanish lessons. Father Olmedo says he expects you to return tomorrow."

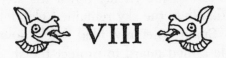 VIII

To the amazement of priests and populace alike, the gods of Anahuac did nothing to avenge the desecration of their most sacred temple. They withheld their wrath while the shrine of Tlaloc, atop the Great Pyramid, was washed clean, the jewels that had once adorned the sides were stripped away and not returned, and the sanctuary hung with garlands of fresh flowers. An altar was erected where the sacrificial stone once stood, and above it was placed a cross made of carved wood and an image of a woman holding a baby.

Chimal was proud to be able to interpret these symbols of the strange religion, and soon every student at the *calmecac* knew the Spanish words for "altar" and "Blessed Virgin." They spoke them in sneering whispers as they watched the Spanish troops, in stately procession, march slowly up the winding steps and kneel in reverence.

Father Olmedo stood behind the altar. From time to time he lifted his hand to make motions in the air, and those in the square could see the movement of his lips. They could not hear his words, for those were drowned by the wild, familiar chant of Huitzil's priests, simultaneously conducting a ceremony in the next shrine.

Since it was Tlaloc whose shrine was violated, and because he was the god of thunder, lightning, and rain, as well as crops, those in the square kept an anxious eye overhead. Surely any moment the blue sky would be blotted out by black clouds and a torrential downpour would sweep the enemy down the steep sides of the pyramid. When the sky remained cloudless and the soldiers of Spain solemnly filed back down, leaving only a single armed guard to protect the shrine, people shook their heads.

"Tlaloc has gone away," they told each other. "He has deserted us. Now the lake and rivers will dry up. The beneficial rains will never fall to nourish our crops, and all men and animals will die of starvation and thirst."

After the twenty days comprising the month of the Raising of the Quetzal Plume Banner had drawn to a close the Aztecs made the familiar amaranth-paste images of the rain god only because they had always done so. The month of the Coming Down of Water would have no significance this year, they thought sadly, for Tlaloc had gone away. Great was their amazement when the rains began as usual, and continued through the ensuing months of Severe Weather and the Toasting of the Corn Supply.

As usual the students of the *calmecac* had an explanation.

"It's because of Lord Cacama," said Quauhtli wisely. "He is gathering an army to attack the invaders. Cuitlahua and several other nobles have joined their forces with his. Tlaloc knows of this, and that is why he is giving us a second chance."

"But Cacama and Cuitlahua cannot order out the army," protested Chimal. "Montezuma is still emperor. The soldiers will obey only him."

"Montezuma is a prisoner. He is not allowed to

78

appear before the people. Therefore he cannot give orders, and the armies know it," Quauhtli pointed out triumphantly.

Chimal knew that this was true. For over three months he had been going to the Palace of Axaya', presumably to study the Spanish language with Father Olmedo, and not once had he laid eyes on the person of his emperor.

He knew that Montezuma was quartered in apartments on the second story, and that a large number of his own people lived there too, in order to serve him. Chimal had spoken to some of them from time to time, and questioned them as much as he dared. Montezuma was well, they said, but very sad. He was completely under the domination of the Spanish leader, Malinche. In only one matter was the emperor remaining firm: he would not forsake his own gods for theirs.

When Chimal reported this to the high priest, Teteoni nodded.

"That was already known to us, but it is good to hear again."

Chimal tried to hide his disappointment. It was hard to ferret out information of which the temple was unaware. Although he did not know who they were, there must be other spies in the palace. So far only one of his own reports had been news: that the Spaniards would depart when they had rebuilt their destroyed water-houses. Teteoni had been excited when he heard that, and in some way unknown to Chimal had managed to do something about it. Aztec carpenters and woodsmen had left shortly afterward for the coast. Under the direction of a Spanish shipbuilder trees were being felled and work was under way on a new fleet.

Chimal was thinking of this today as he left the

temple enclosure and crossed to the palace gates. It had been three months since his report on the destroyed water-houses; if he didn't turn up something of value before long, Teteoni might decide that he was useless as a spy and order him back to the study and penance of the *calmecac*.

The guards at the gate knew him now, and passed him through without question. Chimal crossed the huge courtyard slowly, his eyes searching for something out of the way. He could see nothing to report. The inevitable cooking fires of the hated Tlascalans burned as always, and some of their warriors kept in practice with a friendly game of archery. A group of Spanish soldiers squatted on their haunches, gambling with cards made from an old drumhead. Jewels and gold that had once belonged to the emperor, or perhaps to some temple storehouse, served as stakes and were spread out in gleaming piles before each player. The Spaniards had now taken over the collection of taxes paid by outlying provinces to the emperor, and although Chimal had no proof, he doubted if much of the tribute found its way to Montezuma.

He made his way to Father Olmedo's little chapel, clean and smelling of candle wax and fresh flowers, and as he drew near, his eyes widened in astonishment. A boy only a little older than himself was sitting on the stone threshold. His skin was pale and his hair was reddish-brown. He wore a yellow jacket trimmed with crimson, and tight-fitting crimson trousers that covered the whole length of his legs and disappeared inside soft leather boots.

As soon as he saw Chimal the boy began to smile, and when he was close enough he said in Aztec, "Greetings."

"Greetings to you," replied Chimal automatically. He could hardly believe his own ears. The boy was unmistakably one of the Spaniards, yet no Spaniard had taken the trouble to learn even a single word of Aztec.

"I am Orteguilla," announced the boy, placing his hand upon his breast. He spoke slowly, as though he had to think one word at a time.

"I am Chimal."

"You Chimal." The boy nodded and smiled proudly. Then slowly, word by word: "You—learn—speak—Spanish. I—learn—speak—Aztec."

Chimal was delighted. He sat down on the stone beside Orteguilla. Father Olmedo came from the scented dusk of the chapel and stood smiling down on them.

"Friends," he said approvingly.

"Father Olmedo wants us to be friends—friends," translated Orteguilla, giving the word in both Aztec and Spanish, to make sure that Chimal understood.

"How did you learn our language?" marveled Chimal.

"I have good teacher," replied Orteguilla proudly. "The emperor Montezuma. I am his page."

"Page?" There was no equivalent of the word in Aztec, so Orteguilla had used the Spanish, and Chimal could not understand.

"I serve him," explained the boy after a moment. "He is a noble man. He is lonely sometimes. It pleases him to teach me his language. Doña Marina told the emperor about you, that you were coming here daily to learn the language. He sent me to meet you. He would know more about you."

Chimal was almost overcome by the honor. To think that the emperor was interested in him, that he actually wished to know more about him!

A moment later he had another thought that was not so pleasant. Perhaps the tale was not true. Perhaps this boy was making the whole thing up. Chimal himself was learning Spanish so that he could be useful as a spy; perhaps Orteguilla was learning Aztec for the same reason. He must be very careful, and guard his tongue at all times. Above all he must not mention the uprising being planned by the lords Cacama and Cuitlahua.

"His Majesty is very kind," he said stiffly.

Father Olmedo began speaking rapidly in Spanish, and Orteguilla turned his head to listen. Chimal listened too, but he could not understand. He never could when the Spaniards spoke with each other. It was only when they slowed down, clearly enunciating every word, the way Orteguilla spoke Aztec, that he could follow a conversation. When they had finished, the priest turned and went back inside the chapel.

"I am to be your teacher today," announced Orteguilla importantly. "And perhaps you will help me too. We can speak one tongue, then the other. Father Olmedo is busy with confessions."

"Confessions?"

"Someone has done wrong," explained Orteguilla kindly. "He is sorry. He will tell Father Olmedo how he has sinned, and the father will pray to God to forgive and pardon him."

"Why, it is the same with us," declared Chimal, grasping the idea at once. "When someone who is wicked is about to die he can confess to a priest who will pray to Tlazolteotl, She Who Eats Filth. For a penance, the goddess will devour all his evil doings."

"It is not the same." Orteguilla looked troubled. "And we must not discuss religion, yours or mine. It is a promise that the emperor Montezuma exacted from me before he sent me to meet you. He does not think that you and I can be friends if we argue about religion. He bids us leave that to the priests."

The emperor's word on all things was law, and Chimal bowed his head meekly. It did not matter anyway. There were far more interesting things to talk about. He wondered what secrets this young Spaniard knew.

Before he could go about questioning Orteguilla, however, one of the confessioners who had been occupied with Father Olmedo stepped out of the chapel and into the sunshine. It was Malinche's favorite lieutenant, Don Pedro Alvarado, and this time Chimal did not start when he caught the gleam of sunlight on the golden hair and beard.

"Ho, Orteguilla!" called Alvarado heartily. He said something more that Chimal could not understand before he lowered his great body to the stones beside them.

Today the Spaniard was not clothed in armor. Instead he wore black and scarlet garments, made in the same fashion as Orteguilla's, but of a soft cloth that was strange to Chimal. Around his neck were chains of heavy gold, studded with sparkling jewels, and before he sat down he paused to tighten a belt about his waist to which was attached a sword in a beautifully decorated sheath.

Chimal could not take his eyes off the sword. It was longer than those used by the Aztecs, and it was made of some kind of metal unknown to the Aztecs.

"This is Don Pedro Alvarado," introduced Orteguilla proudly. "He is a great warrior."

"I know," agreed Chimal. He looked past the page, and found the blue eyes staring at him. Alvarado did

not look cruel today; perhaps he was at peace, following his confession to Father Olmedo.

Chimal found courage to ask the question that had been bothering him, but to be safe he phrased it in the Aztec tongue.

"Would Tonatiuh be angry if I asked what metal was used to make his sword?" He spoke slowly, as Orteguilla had done when addressing him. "I have never seen one like it."

"It's Damascus steel," answered Orteguilla promptly, leaving Chimal as much at sea as before. The page turned to Alvarado and spoke in Spanish, but very slowly so that the other boy could understand. "My friend admires your sword."

Alvarado laughed, and promptly drew it from the scabbard, extending it across Orteguilla's lap so that Chimal could feel the point. He said something that the page obviously refused to translate, for the boy shook his head firmly and looked a little indignant. After a moment Alvarado said something else, and this time it met with Orteguilla's approval.

"Don Pedro asks if you would like to be a soldier."

"More than anything," agreed Chimal instantly. His face grew wistful as he added, "But I don't think I ever can be. They say I must be a priest."

When Alvarado heard this he laughed again, but there was something close to sympathy in his blue eyes. He spoke with Orteguilla for a few minutes, and what he said must have concerned Chimal, for he kept looking at the Aztec boy and smiling encouragingly. Then he stood up and sauntered away.

"What did Tonatiuh say?" asked Chimal anxiously, when he was out of earshot.

"He likes you," declared Orteguilla emphatically. His

explanation was half in Aztec, half in Spanish; but Chimal managed to follow. "And that is strange, for Don Pedro thinks first of himself. You impressed him with your answer. He says if you want to be a soldier, do not give up hope. Do not let anything stand in your way. When he himself was young he was sickly, and small for his age besides. He too was advised to go into the priesthood, or to follow some calling that did not require great physical strength. But he did not give up. He worked to develop his muscles and at feats of arms. And one day he began to grow. He grew until he is as you see him now. He says if you do not give up, you may grow too."

Chimal looked after the retreating figure in black and scarlet with a sense of experiences shared. Even if it was only a Spaniard, it was nice to know that someone else hadn't wanted to be a priest.

Orteguilla stood up, smoothing down the rich fabric of his blouse.

"I must go now," he announced. "The emperor may require my services."

"I hope you will come again," said Chimal impulsively.

"I will," promised Orteguilla. "Whenever I can be spared. And perhaps someday Montezuma will allow me to bring you to his apartments. I told you he was most curious about you."

"Oh, do you think so?" cried Chimal breathlessly. This was the most exciting thing that had happened yet. He could hardly wait to return and tell Teteoni. With such prospects, there would be no thought of returning him to the routine of the *calmecac*.

Orteguilla did not hear him. His face was turned toward the slowly opening palace gate, and his eyes were squinting as he tried to make out the members of the company that came marching through.

"They're bringing in some prisoners," he said. "I wonder who they can be."

Chimal too looked toward the gate. A moment later he had forgotten all about the possibility of seeing the emperor.

Guarded by lines of armed soldiers, two men were shuffling across the square. Their progress was impeded by the heavy chains that bound their ankles close together. More chains were about their necks and arms. Chimal recognized them both. They were Cacama, Lord of Tezcuco, and Montezuma's brother, Cuitlahua, Lord of Iztapalapan.

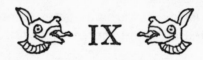 IX

With the capture of the lords Cacama and Cuitlahua, the morale of the *calmecac* sank very low. The students had hoped for an uprising against the Spanish, but without a leader even a small segment of the army would not move. They moped, and Chimal was glad to be able to escape to the Palace of Axaya' each afternoon.

He saw Orteguilla almost every day, for Montezuma took a siesta following his largest meal, and the page was free while the emperor slept. Although the Spanish boy was friendly, he would not discuss the imprisonment of Cacama or Cuitlahua.

"It is better that we do not speak of such things, Chimal," he insisted. "You and I are friends. Let us try to stay that way."

Nor had he, as yet, kept his promise about taking the Aztec to visit the emperor.

One day as the two boys were sitting on the sunny threshold of the chapel the outer gates swung open to admit twenty Spanish men of arms and six Indian porters, bent low beneath heavy burdens. By the way their *maxtlatls* were tied, and by the shells ornamenting the carrying bands they wore about their heads, Chimal recognized the latter as natives of the sea-coast province of Cempoalla, but the soldiers were strangers.

They were known to Orteguilla, however, and the page jumped to his feet.

"Why, they're Sandoval's men!" he cried, as though that should explain everything.

"Who is Sandoval?" Chimal stood up too.

"Lieutenant Sandoval. Cortés left him at La Villa Rica, one of our settlements on the coast. Only last week I heard a rumor—" He stopped, his voice choked with laughter.

By this time the procession had advanced across the square so that is was possible to see the burdens on the porters' backs. Each was stooped under the heavy weight of a fully grown man, trussed up and tied with ropes so that they looked like so many bales of goods. Not one could wave his arms or bend his legs; only the faces were left free to stare upward to the sky. And those faces were white!

Everyone else seemed to be sharing Orteguilla's amusement, for the courtyard rang with shouted jeers and laughter. The Tlascalans, although they did not understand any more than Chimal, laughed too, pointing dirty fingers at the prisoners.

When the porters and guards had disappeared inside the archway leading to the quarters of Cortés, Chimal tugged at Orteguilla's sleeve.

"Those men—were they sick?"

"No." Orteguilla sank down weakly on the stones. He had laughed so hard that there were tears in his eyes, and for a few moments he could not speak. Chimal waited patiently.

"We had heard rumors that an expedition had landed near our settlement of Vera Cruz," explained Orteguilla finally. "It was led by a man named Narvaez, and it was sent by the governor of Cuba to seize Cortés and send him home in irons."

Chimal felt a stir of hope. Malinche had other enemies! Perhaps if he could find out about them, they and the Aztecs might work together. He tried to keep his face expressionless, his voice calm. "Why should anyone want to do that to Malinche?" he asked. "Are these men also Spaniards?"

"Oh, yes." Orteguilla nodded. "It's jealousy. Cortés is doing well. He already has taken more treasure than —" He stopped short, realizing what he was saying. Then he put out his hand and covered Chimal's awkwardly. "Don't get your hopes up," he said honestly. "Narvaez would be just like Cortés. Maybe worse. It's something that had to happen to your people sometime, Chimal. You can't stop it. Neither can I. The thing to do is to submit."

Chimal closed his lips, tightly shutting out all the things he wanted to say. The Aztecs would never give up. They would bide their time, and when the gods gave the signal—providing the emperor was still a prisoner and unable to do so—they would rise and drive out the enemy.

"If the rumor is correct, Narvaez has a big force," continued Orteguilla cautiously. "But he doesn't have the Tlascalans. And he isn't as smart as Cortés. How Sandoval got hold of those six prisoners he sent us, tied up like bags of cabbage, I don't know. But it means that his fort is holding tight. Cortés will know what to do."

"I see," said Chimal stiffly. He stood up, realizing that he must get this information to Teteoni as quickly as possible. "I think I'd better go back. I don't feel very well."

"It's the altitude." Orteguilla nodded with swift understanding. "Sometimes it makes me a little dizzy too."

Teteoni listened carefully to everything Chimal had to report. For the second time his information had been news. At least, the temple had not yet heard of the arrival of the six white prisoners, humiliatingly delivered on the backs of men of burden. However, fleet-footed runners, working in relays, had already reported the arrival of new water-houses on the coast. There were eighteen in all, enough to transport every Spaniard in the country. The priests had been offering prayers and sacrifices in the hope that the intruders would now leave, without waiting for the completion of their new vessels. But the news brought by Chimal suggested that the gods had another plan in mind. Perhaps the Spaniards would fight and destroy each other.

"How many men came with this new expedition, honored uncle?" asked Chimal curiously. It was unlike Teteoni to speak so freely, to exchange information for information. It was almost as though he had forgotten that the boy was still there.

"Nine hundred. And there are four hundred of them already here." The high priest sighed. Then he came to with a start, realizing that he had been thinking aloud. He frowned and said sternly, "Return to your lessons. All this time spent at the palace puts you far behind the others. You must work twice as hard to catch up."

That was untrue, thought Chimal indignantly, bowing his way from the room. He was up with the others in all his studies, for he went to the palace in the afternoons, which the *calmecac* devoted to menial tasks:

cutting wood for the sacred fires, cleaning the temple grounds, and gathering maguey leaves for penance.

On the following morning the old priest who conducted the class on reckoning led his students into the temple square, beside the great calendar stone. Chimal listened intently to his lecture. This was the boy's favorite subject. It had to do with time and the study of the eras of the world. So far there had been four of these eras, each of which had ended in catastrophe.

First the sun had been destroyed by jaguars, and in the darkness all the people save a single pair had been eaten by wild beasts. The second sun had been swept away by wind, again leaving a single couple to repopulate the world; the third sun by fire; the fourth by flood; and the fifth, or present sun, was destined to be swallowed by an earthquake. It was necessary to know about these things. No one knew, of course, just who would be the two fortunate survivors, but they must be warned beforehand of their responsibility to the future world.

It was early, and a chill wind tugged at the priest's thin cotton robes and matted hair. Even so, Chimal thought jealously, he was more fortunate than his students, who were permitted only a *maxtlatl*. Their bare arms and backs were covered with goose pimples, and the chattering teeth on either side of him formed a staccato accompaniment to the thin, piping lecture of the old man.

Suddenly he stopped speaking, and the dark, scarred face wrinkled in anger. One of the young priests had come up to the group and was signaling permission to speak.

"This is an important class," snapped the instructor. "By whose order do you interrupt?"

"By order of the high priest of Coatlique. He bids you dismiss the student Chimalpopoca, who is to go straightway to the Palace of Axaya'."

"Go, Chimalpopoca," commanded the old priest crossly. He scowled at the young man who had interrupted his lecture. "And you go too. There is much to learn, and little time to learn it."

Chimal bowed, and, followed by the envious eyes of the other students, crossed the square to the temple gate. He could not understand why Teteoni had ordered him to go to the palace in the morning. Father Olmedo would not be expecting him so soon.

The guards at the gate were not those usually assigned there, and although they recognized Chimal, they did not stand back to let him enter.

"Father Olmedo is not here," said one of them gruffly. "He has gone away."

"But he will return?" asked Chimal anxiously. If Father Olmedo left permanently, he would have to find another excuse for coming here.

The guard misread his concern, and laughed as he said to the other, "Father Olmedo is making a convert of this one." His voice when he addressed Chimal again was not so gruff. "Yes, boy, he will return. He left with Cortés this morning. But he'll be back. It will take only a few weeks."

A few weeks! Chimal made no effort to hide his disappointment.

"Doña Marina?" he asked quickly.

"She always goes with Cortés," said the second guard. "Someone must translate that heathen tongue of yours."

Chimal forced his voice to a humble note, but inside he was fuming with indignation.

"I am studying your own beautiful language. That is why I come here every day. Father Olmedo helps me. And so does my friend Orteguilla."

"He's telling the truth." The first guard nodded good-naturedly. "I've seen him with the page. Let's let him through."

"No." The second man rattled his arms threateningly. "Don Pedro Alvarado said to admit no one, and he is in charge while Cortés is gone."

At that moment the gate swung open from within, and Alvarado himself, leading a small company of horsemen, rode through. Both guards sprang to attention.

"Tonatiuh! Please, sir. A favor." Chimal called out quickly, addressing Alvarado by the name the Aztecs called him.

"Ah, the would-be soldier!" White teeth flashed in the golden beard. Alvarado pulled on his reigns, glancing down at the boy.

"Please, sir, I would like to ask a favor," said Chimal again. He spoke slowly, carefully pronouncing each Spanish word. He had been making good progress, and every day they seemed to come a little easier.

"What is it?" asked Alvarado grandly.

"Each day I come here. I study your language with Father Olmedo, and sometimes with Orteguilla. I think it is important, for sometime I can be of use as an interpreter, like Doña Marina. Now they tell me that Father Olmedo has gone away. I may forget what I have learned. Please, have I your permission to keep up my studies with my friend Orteguilla?"

"Why not?" Alvarado grinned good-humoredly. "A small boy can do no harm. And, as you say, you may be useful to us sometime." He spoke to the guards.

"Pass him through the gates, and have someone take him to the page."

The soldier who was delegated to escort Chimal conducted him up the stairway leading to the second story of the palace. He seemed quite matter-of-fact about it, as though this were just an ordinary flight of stairs, but Chimal could hardly suppress his excitement. The golden-shod feet of his emperor had touched each one, and at the top His Royal Majesty was residing even now. It was presumptuous for a common subject, such as he, to venture so close, especially without an invitation, but there was no turning back now.

Surrounding the apartment was a garden, similar to those surmounting the roofs of the single-story buildings, but it seemed to Chimal that here the greenery was more verdant, the flowers more sweetly scented. He had no time to look around, for the soldier, standing on the top step, raised his voice in a bellowing roar.

"Orteguilla!"

Chimal shivered. Such a breach of good manners! No well-bred Aztec would dream of screaming like that in private, but this barbarian thought nothing of doing so in earshot of the emperor himself. What was even worse, he did it again!

There came an answering cry from inside the apartment, and a second later the page appeared in the open doorway.

"Chimal!" he exclaimed happily, advancing to meet his guest. "How did you get here?"

"I brought him. Don Pedro's orders." It was the soldier who answered, for Chimal was still too shaken to speak. He kept wondering what other affronts his emperor had been made to suffer.

96

"Alvarado?" Orteguilla smiled widely. "I told you he liked you, Chimal. While Cortés is away perhaps you can come here often. Cortés would never agree to it. He was afraid of spies, you see, but Don Pedro is afraid of nothing. Maybe you can come sometime when the emperor is here."

"Montezuma is not here?"

"No. He escorted Cortés and the troops to the city gate this morning. He'll return this evening. Didn't you know?" Orteguilla was chattering along happily. "That was so all the Aztecs would realize that Montezuma favored our side in the battle."

"I don't understand," admitted Chimal weakly. What a relief to know that the emperor's ears had not been offended by loud voices!

"Cortés is going to the coast," explained Orteguilla swiftly. "He's going to fight Narvaez—you know, the man I told you about yesterday."

"But Malinche did not take all the soldiers," objected Chimal, remembering back to when he had crossed the square. Now that he thought of it, the force *had* seemed smaller than usual. "Won't he need them if he's going to fight a war?"

"He took about two-thirds," said Orteguilla carelessly. "Alvarado has to keep some here, you know—in case anything happens. But I don't think it will. And Cortés will be joined by others—Sandoval and his men from Villa Rica, and Lieutenant de León, from the colony on the gulf. Besides, the Chinantlas have offered to send several thousand natives. They don't get along with the Aztecs, I understand, any more than the Tlascalans." He looked at Chimal curiously, waiting for an answer.

"No," agreed Chimal soberly. "We are enemies."

Anahuac had so many enemies. And a good many conquered provinces, who now paid tribute, would ask
nothing better than a chance to get out from under
Montezuma's tax rolls.

Orteguilla put the thoughts of enemies and war from
his mind.

"Come in. Come in," he urged hospitably. "While
the emperor is away is a good time to show you the
temporary palace."

Even without the presence of Montezuma, the quarters that he occupied filled Chimal with speechless
awe. Most of the furnishings had been brought from the
emperor's own palace, and the walls had been hung
with rich tapestries made of embroidered cotton
or featherwork mosaic. He did not sit upon piles of
mats, as did the common people, but upon a low chair.
It was made of wickerwork brushed with gold, and it
had a back that extended higher than the royal head,
and was slightly slanted to relax the royal spine. The
seat was cushioned with down. His bed was raised
from the floor also, and laid on a frame decorated with
gold, and there were low tables, on which his meals
were served, and handsomely adorned screens to protect him from drafts.

One large room contained nothing but the emperor's
wardrobe. It was filled from wall to wall with rows of
jewel-studded chests holding *maxtlatls* of finest cotton
and rich *tilmatlis*, heavy with embroidery and precious
gems. Montezuma never wore the same garment twice,
and Chimal wondered to whom the discarded cloaks
and loincloths went now that the emperor was permitted so few attendants.

"But this is the room I like best," said Orteguilla,
pulling him along.

He stopped before an open doorway that had been covered by woven net and urged Chimal to press his face close to the lacy screen. Inside, the room had been converted into a miniature forest, with trees and shrubs growing in containers. Their branches thrust upward to the net-covered, open ceiling, and birds of every description flew freely in the morning sunlight. There were rainbow-hued parrots, golden pheasants, scarlet cardinals, and darting hummingbirds, besides other rare but brilliantly plumaged birds that Chimal could not even name.

"This is only a little part of the aviary he has in his own palace," claimed Orteguilla. "It's all they could let him bring. There wasn't room here for any more. But the emperor says he has another room at home filled with nothing but birds of prey, vultures and eagles."

Chimal's eyes grew round with wonder, and Orteguilla, pleased at the impression he was making, continued.

"Besides that, he has a menagerie at home. Wild animals, like jaguars and ocelots. And a snake house, with every kind of snake you can imagine. And ponds, some filled with fresh water, some with salt, containing every variety of fish that swims." He shook his head sadly. "It's too bad he can't keep them."

"Why can't he?" demanded Chimal in surprise. The emperor could do anything.

"Well, for one thing, the cost," admitted Orteguilla, growing a little red. "Why, it takes five hundred turkeys a day just to feed the vultures and eagles alone. And two thousand men, who could be working in the mines, are needed to take care of all those birds and animals and fish. Cortés won't stand for it long."

Chimal closed his lips quickly to keep back a sharp retort. Was Malinche so certain of victory over the newly arrived enemy on the coast? Oh, if there were only a leader, someone to unite the armies of Anahuac against the invaders! But only the emperor could do that, and he had accompanied the enemy to the gates as proof of his favor. Chimal turned away from the page to hide the misery in his eyes.

"I can't stay long today," he said. "I'd better go now."

Teteoni would be anxiously awaiting his report.

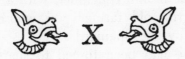 X

Cortés left Tenochtitlán during the month of the Beginning of the Rains, and if the priests had seethed under him, they were openly outraged now that Alvarado was in charge. For one of his initial orders was to prohibit human sacrifice.

That first bloodless day all the people shivered while they awaited the wrath of the gods. They were surprised that the sun rose at all, and when it did, they kept their eyes turned heavenward, each moment expecting the shining ball to crash to the ground, consuming man and beast, forest and city to an ash. At sunset they looked at one another in amazement, sharing the knowledge that the end was but postponed a little. It could come at any moment.

The priests were now speaking openly against the white intruders. They urged the armies to rise. Now, if ever, was the time. Only a hundred and forty Spaniards, with their Tlascalan allies, remained behind the palace walls. But the priests were not military leaders, and the army moved only on command of the emperor.

The month of Bean Porridge opened with ceremonial baths taken by all the populace in the rain-swollen lake. People danced because it was expected that they do so, but their feet went through the motions without gladness. The students of the *calmecac* complained among themselves of hunger, for the priests fasted even more than usual and the school rations of maize cakes were cut in half, and some days stopped altogether. The month concluded with a special rite to Tlaloc, the grim old farmer god whose temple had been defiled by the Spaniards.

Although he had been forced to share the Temple of Huitzil, Tlaloc had been forgiving. He had not withheld the rains, nor had he sent them in such torrents that the young plants had been washed away. The Aztecs were grateful, and the priests resolved to make this feast to Tlaloc one that would show their deep appreciation. A delegation called upon Alvarado with certain requests, and, to his surprise and pride, Chimal was ordered to act as interpreter.

The commander received them in the quarters of Cortés, which he occupied during his superior's absence. He was wearing his black and scarlet costume, and about his neck hung a golden chain set with jade that had once adorned an Aztec god. His blue eyes seemed amused when he saw Chimal, slight and small, in the towering midst of the somber-robed priests.

"Well, boy," he said, "you are proving useful, and even earlier than we thought. What do the black-hearted villains want?"

Chimal had been told what to say, and had already prepared a speech to make certain that he knew all the Spanish words. He explained about Tlaloc's having given up his temple to the strange god, and asked permission that it be returned to him for a single day so that his people would accord him the proper honor.

Even before he finished Alvarado began to frown.

"I have already said that there must be no more sacrifices."

"Not men," said Chimal quickly. "But perhaps one ocelot or jaguar? You see, it is a very special day, Tonatiuh. The highest nobles in the land will come from great distances to perform the sacred dances for Tlaloc. It is no ordinary feast."

"The highest nobles?" repeated Alvarado thoughtfully. "You mean your leaders? How many of them?"

Chimal conferred hastily with Teteoni.

"Six hundred, perhaps a thousand. And it's only for one day. Your god will be returned to the temple as soon as the ceremonies are over. It would mean a great deal if you'd say yes."

"Then I will!" Alvarado made up his mind quickly. "I will give the order to remove our altar and the Blessed Virgin. You may hold your feast."

Chimal flushed with happy triumph, and hurried to tell the stern-faced priests that they had been successful. Tonatiuh had said yes. But there was one thing more that he had been told to ask.

"They would like the emperor Montezuma to be allowed to attend the ceremony," he said, and was not surprised when Alvarado's face darkened and he shook his head.

Chimal had known that this request would be denied. Even he, whom Tonatiuh seemed to favor, had never been permitted to visit the second-story apartment after that first time. He was required to wait at the bottom of the steps for Orteguilla.

All Tenochtitlán seemed to take heart at the news that their god was returning to his own temple, for even a single day. And Tlaloc too seemed pleased, for the gentle rains continued every day, soaking the black soil, swelling the lakes and rivers, cleansing the world.

The older boys at the *calmecac* were especially delighted, for some of them had been chosen to take part in the dance. Chimal's friend Quauhtli was disconsolate because he was not one of these.

"It isn't fair," he protested. "This year I was supposed to be allowed to dance."

"It's because there are so many great lords coming," reasoned Chimal. "They're coming from far distances to honor Tlaloc. There won't be room inside the Wall of Serpents for everyone who wants to be there."

"Then they ought to stay home, those distant lords," snapped Quauhtli. "If it was an ordinary year they'd pay their respects to Tlaloc in one of the smaller temples in their own villages. My father isn't coming. He will do honor to the god, as he always does, in our temple at home."

The dance was to be held in the afternoon, but by mid-morning most of the participants had arrived. They streamed through the gates, dazzling in their most magnificent costumes. Their mantles were of featherwork sprinkled with precious jewels, and their necks, arms, and legs were loaded with collars and bracelets of gold. On their heads they wore the feathered *panaches*, which made each man seem taller, of a hero's height.

In honor of the god the priests had declared a holiday from lessons, and the students were permitted to roam the temple square. However, they had strict orders to stay out from underfoot and away from the Wall of Serpents that surrounded the Great Pyramid.

"Much good this freedom will do us later on," grumbled Quauhtli. "Once they go inside the gates we can't see anything."

He and Chimal were sitting on the lower steps of

104

Coatlique's pyramid, watching the brilliant, multi-colored crowd.

"You can see the priests on Tlaloc's temple."

"Who wants to see the priests?" demanded Quauhtli sulkily. "It's the dancers I want to see. Look, even the Spaniards are coming. And I'll bet they go right inside the Wall of Serpents too."

There were indeed a great number of visitors from the Palace of Axaya' present. No one had noticed them arrive, for they had not marched in together. They were scattered throughout the milling crowd in small groups of three and four, and because the sky was overcast, their armor looked dull and gray. It was hardly noticeable against the brilliant feathered mantles and *panaches* of the Aztec nobles.

"I suppose they've come to make sure that the priests keep their promise about the sacrifice," decided Chimal. He stood up, for the Spaniards had reminded him of his own responsibility. "I've got to go now. It must be almost noon."

"Go? Where are you going?" asked Quauhtli in surprise.

"Where I always go. To the palace."

"But this is a holiday. You can't be expected to go there today. Why didn't you ask that Spanish boy to come here instead? I'd have liked to meet him," admitted Quauhtli curiously.

"I did ask him," said Chimal. "And at first he said yes. He seemed very pleased about it. But the next day he told me that when he asked for permission, Tonatiuh said no. He said that Orteguilla couldn't come here, and that I was to go there today, as usual. Orteguilla said he was very insistent about it too."

"He's selfish!" accused Quauhtli sneeringly. "Tona-

tiuh wants you to miss the festival, but you notice that he and his soldiers are all here."

The priests guarding the gates of the Wall of Serpents were letting people inside as Chimal crossed the square, and the nobles were filing through. Quauhtli was right, he observed, for the Spanish soldiers, their swords banging against their armor, were elbowing their way through the crowd. Obviously they intended to watch from inside the walls. It was unjust. The Spaniards were attending out of curiosity. They were taking up room that could have been filled by Tlaloc's people, who wanted to do him honor.

Today, instead of the usual sentries, the palace gates were guarded by Tlascalans. Although they admitted him without question, Chimal found their presence a little strange. Both Cortés and Alvarado were particular about the outer gates. But an even greater surprise awaited him within. There was not a single soldier visible in the great courtyard. Where could they have gone? Those he had seen in the temple grounds would account for a few, but was it possible that all one hundred and forty men had gone to watch the festivities? Now that he thought of it, there had been a great many small groups scattered through the crowd.

Chimal felt uneasy and wondered if he should return immediately and report the matter to Teteoni. Then he decided against this. The high priest would not be interested in vague suspicions.

When he whistled from the bottom of the steps Orteguilla heard him at once and came running down.

"I'm glad to see you!" he exclaimed. "You're all right?"

"Of course." Chimal looked at him in surprise. "Why shouldn't I be? Is something wrong?"

"Certainly not. It's just that I've been waiting for you. You're late. And with all those strange nobles over there—they could have started something, a battle, perhaps, and there you'd be. It's always the innocent bystander who gets hurt."

"But they're not here for that!" Chimal looked at his friend in amazement. "They came to do honor to Tlaloc, not to fight."

"But they came armed," insisted Orteguilla. His face grew very pink. "We heard that they were bringing all their weapons."

"They brought no weapons. This is a feast to Tlaloc. He is not a war god."

"Oh." For a moment the page looked thoughtful. Then he seemed to put the matter from his mind. "Well, that has nothing to do with us. I have a surprise for you. Don Pedro says we are to have a feast of our own, you and I. I hope you haven't eaten?"

"No," grinned Chimal, rubbing his empty stomach. Yesterday had been a fast day, and there would be no food in the *calmecac* until after the dances were finished this afternoon. He realized that he should observe this regulation along with the others, but he was a guest in someone's house. When your host offered you food it was impolite to decline.

"We're to use Doña Marina's quarters," explained Orteguilla, leading the way. "She's not here, and even if she were she wouldn't mind."

Although the apartment of Doña Marina in no way rivaled the luxury of that occupied by the emperor, Chimal thought it very grand. The walls were hung with cotton tapestries, and the stacks of mats upon which they sat were of the finest weaving.

The meal was served on dishes of carved wood,

beautifully painted, and he had never tasted such delicious food. There were roast venison served in its own juices; turkey cooked with chocolate; hare stewed with honey and spices; a white fish covered with a sauce of peppers and tomatoes; and instead of maize cakes or tortillas, crusty rolls and thin wafers that dissolved in the mouth. There were several vegetable dishes—corn and squash and others that Chimal could not even recognize by name—and, for dessert, sweetmeats and pastry, followed by a great basket of assorted fruit.

Chimal ate until he could not swallow another bite. Then he leaned back and patted his stomach, which felt like a hard, round melon.

"That was a real banquet," he said admiringly.

"Montezuma eats well." Orteguilla smiled.

"Montezuma?"

"The food was all left over from his dinner. The cooks never know what will please his fancy, so they prepare fifty or sixty different dishes. It's all put down before him, and he chooses what he wants. The rest is given away."

Chimal shook his head with wonder. To think that he had partaken of royal food! He wondered what the emperor had selected today in preference to all the luscious things he himself had eaten.

"Why don't we go up on the roof?" he suggested. "Parts of it overlook the Great Pyramid. Maybe we can see some of the dancing."

"No," objected Orteguilla loudly. Then he smiled, as though to apologize for his abruptness. "Not just yet. I've eaten too much to move. Besides, it's begun to rain again."

"Yes," approved Chimal, glancing through the open doorway. "Tlaloc must be happy with his festival.

Orteguilla, where are all the Spanish soldiers today? I didn't see any in the courtyard."

The page shrugged his shoulders and deliberately changed the subject. It was his usual way of avoiding matters that he was not permitted to discuss.

Chimal stayed at the palace longer than usual. Montezuma had excused his page from regular duties that afternoon, and Orteguilla tried in every way to detain his friend. They played a game of ball, then tried their skills at archery, using some of the bows from the soldiers' storehouse. But at last Chimal insisted that he must go, and Orteguilla walked with him to the gate.

"No matter what happens, you and I are friends," insisted the page soberly. Then he grasped the Aztec's arm, pulling him back and out of the way.

The gates were swinging open, and through them poured a great horde of Spanish soldiers. They were in good humor, and their shouts and laughter were flung against the thick stone walls, bouncing back in echoes. As he looked at them Chimal felt himself grow cold with horror, for almost every man wore atop his armor a mantle of featherwork mosaic, and on his helmet a *panache* of tall, brilliant plumage. Gold chains dangled from every neck, and sword hilts protruded a distance from scabbards, for the blades had been loaded with arm and leg bracelets before being thrust back into place.

"Orteguilla!" Chimal gasped.

"Your nobles came armed." The page's tone was defensive. "It was kill or be killed."

"They didn't! I saw them. There wasn't a weapon among them."

Chimal stared at the other boy with loathing.

Orteguilla had known this was going to happen. He had deliberately kept Chimal here, out of the way, while the slaughter was going on. And only a moment before, he had presumed to say that they were friends.

They could never be friends. Never! Chimal turned and ran toward the slowly closing gate, managing to squeeze through just before it was slammed shut.

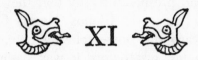

XI

"You mean, you watched it all from the top of Coatlique's pyramid?" Chimal stopped short in the path, and his eyes grew round.

"After you left, the priests all came down," said Quauhtli. His tone was dull, expressionless. "So I went up. I could see inside the Wall of Serpents. I saw—everything. We'd better keep walking. If we fall behind, the priests will be angry."

They were the last of a long line of students who had been assigned the duty of bringing wood for the funeral pyres. It would take a great deal of wood to make over six hundred fires. They must be kept separate, for the ashes of each noble must be returned to his own family.

Chimal was glad that he had been assigned to the wood detail. Some of the students were helping the priests as they wrapped the bodies in winding sheets, together with special amulets and charms. He wouldn't have cared for that assignment.

There had been so much confusion when he returned to the temple that at first he could not find the students of his own *calmecac*. People were running this way and that. Some of them were wailing, others were making threats against the invaders who had committed the massacre, a few had already begun on useful tasks, such as carrying jugs of water to clean the gory enclosure within the Wall of Serpents.

Then Chimal had seen Quauhtli, whose face was blanched greenish-white and whose eyes seemed glazed, as though they had looked on too much horror. Chimal had run over to him, but there had been no time to talk, for one of Coatlique's priests called to them to start for the forest immediately. For the first mile Quauhtli would not speak. He plodded along silently, his eyes on the rain-soaked ground. Then he began to talk in this dead monotone so unlike his usually gay voice. He had witnessed the whole massacre from the top of Coatlique's pyramid, and had been powerless to help.

"Wasn't even—even *one* of them saved?" Chimal shivered, partly from the cold rain, partly from the thoughts that filled his mind.

"No," said Quauhtli flatly. "They had just begun the dance. The greatest nobles, and the oldest, were in the center. Those from the school were on the outside. The Spaniards were against the wall. There were many Spaniards."

"I know." Chimal nodded miserably. Why, oh, why hadn't he returned immediately to report to Teteoni when he had first sensed something wrong?

"All of a sudden the Spaniards shouted. They ran forward with their swords in their hands. They struck the students first, because they were on the outside, and I saw them fall down. I could do nothing."

"Better not think of it," advised Chimal, but his throat had grown so tight that he could hardly say the words.

"Some of the nobles ran toward the gate," continued Quauhtli. "And the soldiers ran them through with their long pikes. And when others tried to climb the wall they were slashed down. I saw it all. When they were all dead the Spaniards began to rob them of their jewels and mantles. It took a long time. After that they opened the gates and went out, and the priests came down from the Great Pyramid, and I came down from the Temple of Coatlique."

Suddenly he began to cry. Tears ran down his cheeks, mingling with the rain, and his body was racked with sobs. Chimal did not know what to do, so he did nothing. They continued to climb the hill side by side, and Quauhtli kept on crying until they reached the woods.

It was after dark when the students returned, each with a heavy burden of wood strapped to his back. They were given bowls of *atolli*, maize porridge, and told to go to bed. Again Chimal felt guilty. This was the first food the others had eaten for two days, while he himself was still so stuffed from the dishes left over from Montezuma's meal that he wasn't hungry. But he was tired, as tired as the other wood gathers, and as soon as he had rolled up in his mat he fell asleep.

He awakened at dawn to the noise of battle. There were the familiar whistles, shrill and penetrating, used by the warriors of Anahuac instead of war cries. There were sounds of crashing rocks, the twang of bowstrings, the purr of arrows, and, a few moments later, the crash of exploding musketry.

Chimal was out of his mat, on his feet, and across the room in an instant. Even so, he was not the first. Students crowded each other to get through the door, with the result that no one could go forward. Then those in front began to push back.

"The high priest! Stand back!"

Teteoni stepped into the crowded sleeping room. He himself had not slept, and his eyes were even more bloodshot than usual, but his lined face beneath the long matted hair was lightened with hope.

"My children," he said hoarsely, "you have work to do. The city is in arms. Every man in Tenochtitlán is here. Before Tonatiuh, the sun god, hides himself this night, the Palace of Axaya' will fall and the nobles who died yesterday will be avenged."

An impolite shout of approval greeted his announcement, but Teteoni let it pass unnoticed.

"Who is the leader, honored sir?" Quauhtli alone dared phrase the question for everyone.

"The gods themselves," declared Teteoni proudly. "No man is leader over all the warriors, although every *telpochcalli* is responsible for its own."

"And how about us? To whom are we responsible in this battle?"

Teteoni shook his head sadly.

"Our young warriors, those who were ready for battle, fell yesterday within the Wall of Serpents. You who are left are still untrained. You will make arrows for the others to use. They will need many. Come."

The younger students of the *calmecac* followed their high priest into the morning. They could hear the sounds of battle floating across the wall. They could almost picture what was going on: some would be attempting to scale the rocks, others endeavoring to set fire to the wooden gates, or to send blazing arrows to the rooftops. The battle was so close, and yet so very far away.

All morning long they sat cross-legged on the ground, doggedly chipping at the hard stones that tipped the warriors' arrows. Their hands grew cramped, but they paused only long enough to flex their fingers before they continued again. Their whetting stones gouged deep gashes in their own skin, but remembering that men were suffering worse than this outside the walls, they ignored the painful cuts.

In mid-morning a young warrior came striding importantly across the square. He wore a padded jacket, made to deflect arrows, and he carried a round wooden shield and a short sword.

"That one's not so much." Quauhtli scowled enviously. "Look, he still wears a *piochtli*. He hasn't yet taken his first prisoner."

"He doesn't look any older than we are," said Chimal wistfully. Then he was on his feet, waving his arms and calling, "Eecatl! Eecatl!"

Eecatl stared; then he began to smile. He forgot that he was a warrior on official business and came hurrying toward them.

"Chimal! When they sent me to the temple I hoped I'd see you. I've been looking for you all morning at the palace wall."

Chimal hung his head in shame.

"They wouldn't let us go. They said we didn't have the proper training."

"But you've been here for months!" Eecatl shook his head in disbelief. "What have you been doing?"

Since the greatest rivalry existed between the *calmecac* and the *telpochcalli*, Quauhtli could not stand the implied slight.

"He's been acting as a spy," he said quickly. "Every day Chimal has been going to the Palace of Axaya' and spying on the Spaniards. Why, he's even learned to speak their language. Has anyone at your school done that?"

"No." Eecatl looked at Chimal with respect.

"And now I make arrow points." Chimal laughed to cover his confusion.

"Somebody has to make them," agreed Eecatl. He grinned. "And somebody has to pick them up after they're made and take them to the experienced warriors. Me."

"How's the battle going?" asked Quauhtli anxiously.

"Several times we've almost stormed the walls. We'll make it yet. We've lost a lot of men, but they've lost some too. I saw at least four Spaniards fall, and I don't know how many Tlascalans."

"I hope they send him again for arrow tips," said Quauhtli after Eecatl had gone. "Not everyone would stop to tell us what's going on. Do you know him very well, Chimal?"

"We studied together for a year under Ocelotl, the old warrior," explained Chimal. "He left for the *telpochcalli* only a week before I came here."

"And already he's allowed to fight!" Quauhtli jabbed so hard at the obsidian that the entire point broke off in his hands. "Maybe we do waste too much time in studies that don't matter."

To their disappointment Eecatl was not sent again to the temple, and they had no further information on the battle raging outside the walls. The hours dragged by. Their stomachs told them that it was long past noon, but no one stopped his work to eat. Their hands were stiff and bleeding now, and their *maxtlatls* stained from using them as towels.

In mid-afternoon the sounds of fighting ceased. The boys looked up from their work and saw that everyone

117

was running toward the gate. The long robes of the priests flapped about their ankles. Students from other *calmecacs* had left their tasks unfinished and were racing after.

"Come on!" called Quauhtli, and the boys of Coatlique's *calmecac* dropped their obsidian fragments on the ground and followed.

There was such a crowd at the gate that they could hardly get through, but somehow Chimal and Quauhtli found a small opening and squeezed outside. The street between the temple and the Palace of Axaya' was jammed with warriors. They stood shoulder to shoulder, and every head was tilted, every eye strained toward the thick, high wall that surrounded the palace. Some of the stones were loosened, Chimal noted with satisfaction. Only a few hours more and there would be a sizable breach. Then his eyes continued on, and he forgot everything else.

The emperor Montezuma was standing on the topmost stones. He was dressed in his finest raiment, and the wind tugged at the vivid feathers of his *panache*, making them stand out about his sallow face like a ruff. The crowd was silent as it gazed upon the emperor, and Montezuma looked sadly back at his people. Then he spoke.

"Go home, my children. You know not what you do. If you continue to besiege the palace Tonatiuh has threatened to lay hands upon my royal person. He will slay your emperor."

He turned and went back down the steps leading to the inner courtyard. After a moment the warriors began slowly filing away.

XII

Although the Aztecs obeyed the pleas of their emperor to halt the siege, they could not forget the massacre of their nobles so easily. Early the next morning the street in front of the palace gates was the scene of new activity, only instead of armed warriors the participants were slaves with digging implements. The pavement was broken up and the soil banked in great mounds before each entrance. To make doubly sure that the enemy would not obtain new supplies, all the markets were temporarily closed. After this, the people settled back to wait for famine to accomplish what Montezuma had prohibited them from doing.

"They've got lots of food," said Chimal, remembering an afternoon when Orteguilla had taken him to see the storehouses, piled high with produce. "But there aren't any springs in the palace, and they'll run out of water pretty soon."

"Good," approved Quauhtli. Then he frowned. "Of course they can always dig a well."

"It won't do any good. Malinche already tried. Maybe he thought that this might happen someday. All the water they could bring up was salt." For some reason it made Chimal a little sad to think of Orteguilla suffering from thirst. Of course the page was one of the enemy, and he hated him for that reason, but he didn't like to think of anyone's being thirsty. "If it starts to rain again, they could catch that and drink it," he suggested hopefully.

"Tlaloc won't send the rain," scoffed Quauhtli. "Why should he help the enemy after everything they've done to him?"

The rains had stopped the morning of the battle. The funeral pyres within the Wall of Serpents blazed brightly day and night, and now that they did not have to obey the edict of Don Pedro, the priests had resumed the daily sacrifices.

The days slipped by until they had made a fortnight, and then a messenger arrived at the temple with the news that Cortés was returning to Tenochtitlán.

"They say he was victorious over his enemies," reported Quauhtli. "And now they've all come over to his side. Malinche has twelve hundred Spaniards instead of just a few hundred, as he had before."

"I wonder what he'll think when he gets back and finds the palace barricaded." Chimal laughed. "But maybe they won't let him through the city gates this time."

"Oh, they'll let him through," Quauhtli insisted. "It's as easy to pen up twelve hundred Spaniards as it is a hundred. The priests have given orders that everyone is to stay off the streets when he arrives. And anyone peeping over his rooftop is to keep hidden."

"He'll think he's marching in to a deserted city. Oh, I wish that we could watch! I'd give anything to see his face."

"We're going to," Quauhtli told him smugly. "There's a spot on top of the temple wall where we can watch. It's right next to the Pyramid of the Sun, and there's a big carving there, so that if one of the priests happens to look down he can't see us."

"Quauhtli!" Chimal gasped. "Do we dare?"

"Of course," said Quauhtli. He grew serious. "It's a secret place, and only the older students of Coatlique's *calmecac* are supposed to use it. But after the Feast of Tlaloc, I guess that's what we are."

Classes were now back to normal, and the boys' greatest fear was that the Spaniards might arrive in the midst of a session so they could not steal away. But they worried needlessly. It took several hours to march troops through a city the size of Tenochtitlán, and the Spaniards arrived in late afternoon.

Chimal had been sweeping the temple steps when Quauhtli came for him. He dropped his broom and followed his friend around the Wall of Serpents to the farther side of the Pyramid of the Sun. Here the outer wall began, blocking the sacred enclosure from the eyes of passers-by. Where the wall joined the pyramid a sprawling vine with scarlet flowers found its way to the top, spilling over the edge to the other side. Quauhtli grasped hold and began climbing at once. After a moment Chimal followed. To his relief the growth was sturdier than it looked, and soon he was on top.

"Lie flat," ordered Quauhtli. "And cover yourself a little with the leaves—just in case."

Chimal did as he was told, then turned his head to look down on the street. It was empty for as far as he could see. He inspected the rough barricade before the gates and the sentry pacing the opposite wall. No one could have asked for a better vantage point.

"Why doesn't the *calmecac* of the sun god use this spot?" he whispered. "It's closer to them than to us."

"It's always belonged to Coatlique's *calmecac*," said

Quauhtli. "I don't know why. Maybe it's always been so. One *calmecac* does not steal from another."

They became aware of high, penetrating sounds that seemed to come from a great distance. Quauhtli's black eyebrows lifted questioningly.

"A bird?"

"No, trumpets." Chimal recognized the sound. "Malinche's coming."

The sounds were increasing, growing in volume as the troops marched through the empty streets. Someone from the palace must have heard them also, for in a few moments a welcoming peal of artillery sounded from within. The boys watched the smoke float up above the walls, dissolving into the pale sky from which Tlaloc withheld the rain. They had grown used to the sounds of cannon and musketry. On the day of the battle those same guns had accounted for no small damage to the temple atop the Pyramid of the Sun.

The trumpets grew louder every minute, but it seemed to take a long time before the troops themselves appeared. As usual the riders led the way, and Chimal, who had by this time lost all fear of the Spaniards' mounts, tried to count them. There must have been a hundred horses, and the solid lines of infantry behind filled the wide street, continuing on around the corner of the temple wall! How was it possible that Malinche with his small force could have defeated such an army?

The advance riders were now close enough so they could see the great mound of rubble heaped before the gate. Cortés lifted his hand, and the signal to halt was passed back along the lines.

"What will he do?" whispered Quauhtli happily.

"Dig it out," said Chimal. "It's all he can do."

A conference between Cortés and two of his lieutenants was going on in the street below. One of them rode back along the lines, and after a time a group of natives came forward and began attacking the barrier. Since they were unequipped for such work, they had to remove the dirt with their bare hands.

"Serves them right," declared Quauhtli in a pleased whisper. "Dirty Tlascalans!"

Eventually the rubble was cleared to one side and the heavy gates swung open. Sounds of welcome rose above the wall as the riders and infantry passed through, blending into the shrill whistles with which the besieged Tlascalans greeted their own returning clansmen.

"There's an awful lot of them," observed Chimal in a worried tone as the last of the painted war-riors pushed and squeezed his way through the slowly closing gate. He had known that there would be over a thousand Spaniards, but he had not expected so many Tlascalan reinforcements. Counting those already in the city, Cortez must have seven or eight thousand native allies at his command.

"With so many to feed, their supplies will go faster than ever," gloated Quauhtli. He motioned with his head toward the street down which the troops had come. "It took them so long to dig their way in that their sick are catching up with them."

Chimal looked over his shoulder. Four natives bear-ing a litter were trotting toward the gate. It was im-possible to see the man under the gray blanket, but he must have been a Spaniard. A wounded Tlascalan chief would have been covered with mats, while a common soldier would have been left behind.

On arriving at the closed gates the porters put down their burden, and one of them pounded for admittance.

There was some delay, but finally the gates were opened enough for the small party to pass through. As they did so, the blanket caught on one of the rough timbers and was pulled off the still figure on the litter. The four bearers, anxious to get inside as quickly as possible, did not stop, and when the gates were slammed shut the blanket lay in a gray heap on the ground outside.

Quauhtli began lowering himself immediately to the street.

"I'm going to get it," he announced gleefully.

"What for?"

"A souvenir. For the *calmecac*." Quauhtli lowered himself as far as he could, then dropped the rest of the way. A moment later he had dashed across the street, scooped up the armload of gray cloth, and was back again below the wall.

"I'll have to go around to the temple gate," he called softly. "I can't climb back up from the outside. You meet me there, and signal when it's safe."

Chimal nodded soberly as he prepared to lower himself by the vine. For some reason that he could not explain, he wished that Quauhtli hadn't taken the blanket from the sick man.

He was the only one who felt that way. The students of Coatlique's *calmecac* received the trophy with delight. The blanket was cut up into squares so that each student could have his own piece, and most of those fragments were divided into smaller sections as their owners shared with friends in other *calmecacs*.

The two boys retold the account of the arrival of Cortés and his troops so many times that Chimal grew sick of it. He was glad when the next day brought a development that made his own story pale by comparison.

Around noon Cuitlahua, Lord of Iztapalapan, who had been seized with Cacama, the Lord of Tezcuco, was set free by the Spaniards. He came walking through the temple gates and was immediately rushed to the high priests of the Great Pyramid. Before long the priests of the other temples were summoned for a conference, and shortly afterward the pulsating voice of a huge signal drum sounded over the city. Since this drum was reserved for momentous occasions, the students of the *calmecacs* looked at each other with anticipation.

"Now we'll hear all about it," said Quauhtli. "Malinche must have some reason for letting Lord Cuitlahua go now when he wouldn't before. My guess is that he wants to be friends. He thinks that by turning loose an important prisoner we'll forget everything that's happened."

"As if we could!" scoffed one of the students. "What a fool he is!"

"Malinche's not a fool," insisted Chimal. "I think he sent Lord Cuitlahua with a message. He couldn't send one of his own people—not even Doña Marina."

Chimal proved to be right. When, in answer to the temple drum, the square was crowded with the populace, Cuitlahua, attended by the priests, descended from the top of the pyramid.

"I have come from the Palace of Axaya', where I was a prisoner of the Spanish dogs." He addressed the people from the lowest flight of stairs, and his voice carried to the outer fringes of the throng below. "Malinche has set me free so that I may bring you a message."

He paused, waiting for the murmur of hatred to pass through the crowd at the mention of the Spaniard's nickname. Chimal studied him closely. There was little resemblance to Montezuma in this younger brother. While the emperor was gentle in nature, and his love of luxury apparent in his dress, Cuitlahua was a seasoned warrior. It showed in the depth of chest below the plain white cotton cloak, in the clenched set of his jaw, the flash of his narrowed black eyes, the rippling muscles in his arms, developed from long practice with the *maquahuitl*. Whatever ornaments or jewels he had worn at the time of his capture had been stripped from his person, but as he stood there in the cotton *maxtlatl* and *tilmatli* of a common man, Cuitlahua was every inch the leader.

"The Spaniards have found a spring, which was unknown to us, within the palace walls," he continued when everything was still. "And while it is small, it provides them with drinking water. But their food is running low. The message sent by Malinche is this: open up your markets, or he will open them for you. What is your answer, men of Anahuac?"

"No. No. Never!" The reply came from every corner of the square. It rose like a huge breaker in the sea, and crashed at Cuitlahua's feet against the base of the pyramid. The Lord of Iztapalapan smiled thinly, but with approval.

"And so say I," he agreed. "I have sent for my nephew, Guatemozin, who although young in years is skilled in warfare. He will assist me, and with your help not one of these Spanish dogs or their Tlascalan allies shall remain alive."

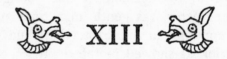

XIII

The effects of Lord Cuitlahua's leadership were apparent to the *calmecac* no later than the following morning. Classes on reckoning, astronomy, and similar subjects were abandoned in favor of instruction in arms. For the first time in several months Chimal found himself with a wooden *maquahuitl* in his hands, and, to his delight, he had not forgotten all Ocelotl's training. In fact he was so far advanced over some of the other boys that the warrior-priest who was instructing the class put him in charge of a small group that was having difficulty in thrusting and parrying blows.

But most of the drill was with the *atatls,* for it had been decided that the students of all the *calmecacs* were to be stationed on one of the flat terraces of the Pyramid of the Sun. There they would have some protection while they discharged their missiles on the street below.

Early in the morning pillars of smoke arose from three directions, for Cuitlahua had ordered all drawbridges that protected the causeways leading to the island city raised and destroyed. Barricades of timber and earth were erected at vantage points along the avenues leading to the Palace of Axaya', and the lake was black with watercraft bringing fighting men to the defense of Tenochtitlán. They came from Iztapalapan and Tlacopan, Tezcuco and Tepeyacac, and when they entered the canals their canoes were joined by those of city men, who lay down their implements of trade and took up arms. Master feather workers came from Tolteca, traders and merchants from Tlatelolco, farmers from Cuepopan, the place of blossoming flowers, and from Moyotlan, in the south, where the canals and streets ended in marshes. Their years as young warriors fresh from the *telpochcalli* were far behind them, but they were not forgotten. Now that he had a leader, each man was prepared to fight for his city.

Cuitlahua gave himself but a single day to prepare for war. At daybreak on the following morning it began.

Standing with the other students at his assigned post on the pyramid, Chimal could see the army coming. They advanced like a strong, relentless tidal wave down every avenue approaching the palace, and like the sea they gave off a roaring sound, the angry mutter of thousands of voices. At the same time all the rooftops overlooking the streets bristled with arms as fighting men stood up, waving their weapons.

Since the pyramid was higher than the wall where he and Quauhtli had watched the return of Cortés, Chimal could see over the battlements across the street and into the palace courtyard. He saw the trumpeter raise his silver bugle to call the enemy to arms. Artillerymen in thick, padded jackets clambered up to the thirteen guns that now surmounted the wall; archers and harquebusiers scurried for the smaller openings in the rock work where stones had been removed to receive the barrels of their muskets. Chimal could see the hated Tlascalans setting their animal-shaped headdresses in place and flourishing *maquahuitls*, and then there was no time to look any more, for the tidal wave of Aztecs was nearing the wall.

What happened next was so terrible that Chimal could scarcely believe his eyes. The guns on the battlements roared, belching smoke and fire, and when the air cleared, all the warriors in the lead lay crumpled in the street.

For a moment the advance was halted. Then those who now held the lead yielded to the pressure of those behind. Exactly what had happened they did not know. They had seen and heard the discharge of artillery before. The Spaniards were accustomed to celebrate their holy days in this manner, but always with harmless results. It was true that in the one-day battle following the massacre of nobles parts of the temple atop the Pyramid of the Sun had been destroyed, but no one had been hurt.

In that moment of indecision the warriors on the rooftops took deliberate aim at the enemy in the courtyard. A rain of arrows poured onto the Spaniards and Tlascalans penned up within the four walls, and stones hurled from a hundred slings wrought even greater damage.

The advancing Aztec forces recovered from their bewilderment and pressed on over the prostrate bodies of their slain comrades under the very muzzles of the guns. Once there, they attempted to scale the walls, but they soon realized that this was useless. The moment a head appeared above the top it was shot down by a harquebusier or lopped off by a Tlascalan *maquahuitl*.

Chimal and his classmates were using their *atatls*, blindly hurling darts and stones. He had no idea whether or not one of his missiles found a mark; there was too much disturbance inside and out. Over the palace walls erupted a continuing sheet of flame and smoke, and the street was so littered with the bodies of the slain that the pavement was scarcely visible.

Burning arrows were shot from rooftops into the courtyard, and while they had no effect on the stone buildings of the palace, the wooden parts of the exteriors and the roofs, as well as the temporary sheds that housed the Tlascalans, soon burst into flames. Chimal glimpsed women and a few men trying to check the fire by throwing earth on it.

The battle continued throughout the day, and the losses were heavy on both sides. Chimal's arms were sore from using the *atatl;* his back ached from bending over to pick up stones for ammunition; and his eyes burned from the smoke. Worst of all were his ears. His whole head ached and throbbed from the sounds of battle, the cries of the dying, and the deafening roar of the cannon. But somehow he kept on.

Night came, and because the Aztecs did not fight after dark Cuitlahua withdrew his forces and sent rescue parties to recover the dead and wounded from the street. The boys of the *calmecac* were so tired when they sat down for their evening meal that their hands could scarcely carry their maize cakes to their mouths.

"I wonder if it will be over tomorrow," said Quauhtli. "They can't keep this up long. They're losing a lot of men."

"So are we," Chimal reminded him.

"But we've got more to lose," Quauhtli pointed out triumphantly.

The next day's battle was much like the first, except that the Spanish cavalry rode out on the street, followed by a large force of infantry and Tlascalans. Here they were not penned up in small quarters. Without the benefit of their artillery, and clearly outnumbered, they were forced to retreat in a few hours to their palace stronghold, but not before they had retaliated for the fires of the day before by setting the torch to a large number of Aztec houses.

On the third day the emperor Montezuma ascended the battlements of the palace. His royal person was protected by the shields of three Spanish soldiers, who held them in such a way that they would deflect any stray arrows, but the shields were unnecessary as soon as the warriors recognized their monarch.

The whistles and cries of the assailants were hushed and a great stillness fell over the Aztecs swarming the street and rooftops. Some of them fell to their knees, their eyes respectfully cast down, but there were others who, for the first time in their lives, stared straight at their ruler. The boys of the *calmecac* on the Pyramid of the Sun were among these.

"Why, he's a man, just like us," murmured one of them in astonishment.

"The Spaniards haven't taken his jewels, anyway!" There was a note of criticism in the second voice.

Certainly Montezuma made a splendid appearance. He was wearing his finest robes. His blue and white cloak flowed from one shoulder where it was held in place by a carved clasp of jade and emeralds of unusual size. On his feet were golden sandals, and on his head the jeweled crown of state. He looked down at his people on the street, then up at those on the rooftops. The soldiers, seeing that all was peaceful, stepped back.

"Why are my children in arms against the palace of my father?" asked Montezuma. His voice was calm, but it carried in the still air so that everyone could hear. "Is it that they think their sovereign a prisoner, and wish to release him? If so, they have acted correctly. But they are mistaken. I am no prisoner. The strangers are my guests. I remain here because I love them."

At this a slow, angry murmur began to run over the crowd.

"Base Aztec," muttered one of the boys close to Chimal.

"Our emperor has turned into a woman!"

"Has he forgotten that bloody day when all the nobles were murdered in the temple?"

Montezuma seemed unconscious of the effect his words were having on the crowd.

"Return to your homes," he ordered. "Lay down your arms. Show respect to me, who has a right to your obedience."

Chimal did not see from which rooftop the stone was hurled, but he heard the sound of its passing. He saw Montezuma stagger, and the jeweled crown tumble from his head. The soldiers hurried forward with their shields, but not before two more stones had struck the battlement beside them.

As the emperor was carried from the wall the Aztecs looked at one another in shocked disbelief. Someone had dared to raise his hand against the sacred person of their monarch, yet there was not one to say it should not have been. They looked to their new leader for direction. When Cuitlahua signaled to continue the battle as before, they obeyed.

By far the greatest damage done to the inmates of the palace was by the five or six hundred warriors stationed on top of the Great Pyramid. It rose to a height of nearly a hundred and fifty feet, and the Aztecs, protected by the sanctuaries, were able to discharge such a torrent of arrows on the garrison that no one could leave his post without the greatest peril. Now that he thought of it, Chimal was sure that the stone which had struck down the emperor must have come from the Great Pyramid; otherwise he, Chimal, could never have heard its passage through the air.

Cuitlahua had known that sooner or later Cortés must attempt to take the stronghold, and he had made careful plans. The stairs leading to the top of the pyramid were barricaded at several points; every warrior had his assigned duty; and the students of the *calmecacs* were told to stay where they were, safely out of the way.

"You'd think we were babies," stormed Quauhtli when he heard the order. "Why are we here, if not to learn to fight?"

"You can't learn with real swords in a real battle," Chimal told him, remembering how poorly most of them had done on their one day of practice. He was glad that he had spent all those months with Ocelotl. Of course it didn't mean that he was very good as yet, but at least he knew how much he had to learn.

"If the older boys were here they wouldn't be so hard on the rest of us," scowled Quauhtli. "It isn't fair."

The attempt to storm the Great Pyramid was made the day after the stoning of Montezuma. Chimal and his friends saw the party, consisting of about a hundred Spaniards, dash through the quickly opened palace gates and down the street to the main gate of the temple. Arrows poured down on them from rooftops, and from behind barricades the Aztecs hurled darts and more arrows. Some of the party fell, but the majority got through.

"Now we can't see anything," complained Quauhtli in disgust as the last man passed through the temple gate. "How will we know what's happening?"

The sloping sides of the Great Pyramid acted as a screen, blocking the whole scene from their view. All they could do was listen, and that wasn't very satisfactory.

After what seemed an interminable time the warriors at the top set up a barrage of jeering whistles, and the boys beamed at each other in triumph. The storming party had been unsuccessful. They tried to count the men who dashed helter-skelter down the street and through the palace gate. All they could tell was that the loss had been heavy.

Later that day another attempt was made. This time the storming party was much larger. Three hundred Spaniards and several thousand Tlascalans came pouring from the palace.

"Malinche's leading this party himself," said Chimal. "And there's Tonatiuh!"

"It won't do any good," claimed Quauhtli stoutly. "Huitzil will stop them. His temple will never fall."

But Huitzil's temple did fall. Despite the rain of arrows, rocks, and burning rafters that the Aztecs sent hurtling down the sides, the Spaniards, fighting every step, slowly mounted the three flights of stairs that led to the top. Here was a wide, flat area, large enough to provide a battlefield for a thousand men. Only the sacrificial stones and the two wooden temples, one to Huitzil, the other to Tlaloc, stood in the way.

The students of the *calmecac*, watching from the terrace, were no longer dependent solely on their ears.

The hand-to-hand battle was being enacted before their eyes. The height of the Great Pyramid made it visible for miles around, and elsewhere in the city those engaged in smaller battles stopped to view this larger one.

The edge of the area was unprotected by parapets, and more than once combatants tumbled off together. It was impossible to run, and neither side asked for quarter. They fought for three hours, and although the Spaniards were outnumbered at the start, they had the advantage of armor and of matchless swords.

When the sun sank behind Chapultepec, the Hill of Grasshoppers, Chimal gave a tired sigh.

"It's over," he said softly. "We've lost."

One after another the Aztec warriors had fallen. Now there remained only the two high priests of Huitzil and Tlaloc, whose black robes flapped in the late breeze as they stood, each protecting the shrine of his god with his own body.

They were not allowed to stand there long. With a shout that rang over the temple grounds the Spaniards pushed the old men out of the way. Then, before the horrified eyes of the onlookers below, they shoved and tugged the two stone images from their places and sent them tumbling over the edge of the terrace.

A great moan burst from the populace, and Chimal, with the other students, fell flat on the ground, burying his face. This was the end of everything, he told himself. The gods had suffered greatly, but this last insult was too much. Now their wrath would descend upon the earth; the world would be destroyed by earthquake as it was written on the calendar stone. Trembling, he waited for a long time. When nothing happened he lifted his head and looked up.

The Spaniards were gone from the top of the Great Pyramid, and so were the two high priests. But the Spaniards had left a memento of their presence. Both of the wooden shrines, which once had housed the gods, blazed brightly, casting an ominous light over the city of Tenochtitlán.

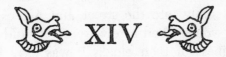 **XIV**

Like Chimal, the other Aztecs anticipated immediate destruction following the insult to their two highest gods. When it failed to occur, they came to the conclusion that Huitzil and Tlaloc expected their people to avenge their honor.

Cuitlahua reorganized his paralyzed forces, and the battles continued. These were no longer confined to the streets around the palace, for Cortés sent his men to fight in the open. Cuitlahua was playing with the enemy, and his greatest ally was time. Every day the Spaniards lost a few more men from hunger and sickness as well as from battle; their provisions and water were low; and without bridges they could not hope to escape. The Aztecs had an unlimited supply of warriors. Their losses had been tremendous, but there were many more who could be called. They had food and water, good health, and they could get around in canoes without depending upon the bridges. Before long they were sure that Huitzil and Tlaloc would be avenged with Spanish blood on their altars.

The month of the Lesser Feast of the Lords slipped by. Even the salters, who usually spent these twenty days in special rites, had been too occupied to give the proper services to their patron goddess of sea water. On the very last day the students of the *calmecac*, who had come to regard their station on the Pyramid of the Sun as a prison, were amazed to see the palace gates swing open and an unusual procession emerge.

These were neither Spaniards nor Talascalans who stepped solemnly into the street, but Aztecs. Many of them were women, and a few were very old men, who by the richness of their cloaks it was easy to identify as nobles. The others were servants, and four of them carried a golden litter on which lay the still figure of a man totally covered by a robe of woven featherwork.

As soon as they had passed through, the gate was slammed behind them, and the little party waited in the street as though uncertain as to what to do next.

The Spanish artillery stopped just before they came out, and now the Aztecs on the rooftops lay down their arms. From the temple wall, where he had been directing the fighting, Cuitlahua, himself, jumped to the street. He was followed immediately by his nephew Guatemozin, and two other nobles. The four men hurried toward the little party that awaited their arrival.

"Is it Montezuma?" asked Quauhtli in an awed whisper. "Is he dead?"

Chimal nodded. That still figure under the woven featherwork could be no one else.

The four nobles took over the litter from the common men who carried it, and the remainder of the party fell in behind. Neither side resumed the battle until they were out of sight.

"I wonder where they're taking him?" asked someone in a small voice. Even an emperor who was in disfavor with his people was royalty.

"To his own palace," guessed another. "Later he'll probably be buried with his ancestors on Chapultepec. It was his favorite summer home."

"Now Cuitlahua will be emperor," decided Quauhtli. "And he'll make a good one."

Two of the boys from Coatlique's *calmecac* were ill the following morning, and one of them was Quauhtli. Both complained of sore throats, and their skin was so hot to the touch that it made Chimal draw back in alarm.

"I'll go and get Citlalcoatl," he offered, referring to the priest who looked after the health of the students.

Citlalcoatl was not pleased at the summons. It was his fourth call that morning, he grumbled. Two other students were complaining of pains, and it was his private opinion that they were growing tired of standing on the Pyramid of the Sun, and merely wanted a vacation. But finally he came, and threw a handful of maize into a bowl of water in order to make his divination of the sickness.

"Just one of the common ailments of children," he decided. "Go to the temple of Iztlilton and drink some of the black water from one of the closed pots you will find there. You will be well by evening."

Quauhtli groaned that he would never make it as far as Iztlilton's temple; he would rather stay here and die.

Chimal, who had been studying his friend closely, called out, "Please look, honored sir! There are red bumps appearing on his chest."

Citlalcoatl grunted and came closer to see for himself.

"So there are. Then this is not what I thought. The divination must relate to the other boy." He turned and pointed a stern finger at the second patient. "You go to Iztlilton's temple and drink the black water. Hurry, before the sickness grows worse."

141

Moaning softly, the boy staggered to his feet and tottered out the door.

"Now as for you," continued Citlalcoatl, turning again to Quauhtli, "if those bumps are ulcers or skin eruptions, they've been sent by the goddess Tzapotlatenan. If it's leprosy, Tlaloc is responsible. We'll have to make a sacrifice to each of them, just to make sure. I will have word sent to your father that he must pay. In the meantime"—he dipped into a leather pouch at his side and brought out a handful of brown leaves—"eat this. It's tobacco. Sometimes it helps bring down certain swellings."

"May I stay with him?" pleaded Chimal. "He's very ill."

"Certainly not." Citlalcoatl frowned. "Your place is on the pyramid with the others. I'll look in on your friend from time to time."

It was the longest day that Chimal had spent on the pyramid, and the most uncomfortable. Tlaloc had grown weary of withholding the rain, and around noon he let it descend in a fine drizzle. Before long the boys were dripping wet, and there was no place on the terrace where they could seek shelter.

"Look, the Spaniards are trying to catch the rain in tubs." One of them laughed. "They're really short of water."

Chimal didn't care. His teeth were chattering, and his bones ached with a growing chill. He was so miserable that by noon he even forgot to worry about Quauhtli. After a while he sat down on the sodden terrace, burying his head in his arms. One of the boys asked if he was sick, and Chimal shook his head. He was only cold, he mumbled, and he wished he were home. The others understood. They too were cold in their cotton loincloth garments.

Because of the overcast sky, darkness came early, and when the priest arrived to tell the youths that it was time to return to their *calmecacs* they forgot their manners and pushed each other to reach the stairs. Chimal was the last one down. His legs shook so that they could scarcely carry him, and he had to cling to the banister to keep from falling.

The priest who was waiting at the bottom looked at him sharply.

"Are you ill, Chimalpopoca?"

He tried to shake his head, and the effort left him so dizzy that he lost his balance. He heard a great ringing in his ears, and a black sky filled with stars whirled past his closed eyelids. He did not know that the priest gathered him up as he fell and carried him across the rainy courtyard to the *calmecac*.

Several times Chimal roused from his stupor. Once it was to the throbbing of the great drum on the pyramid. It went on and on, and he seemed to sense that the other boys, who had been sleeping all around him, were awake and rushing from the room. Another time it was to the sound of muffled shouts and whistles. Much later he thought he heard the voice of his uncle, the high priest, giving sharp orders, but to whom he neither knew nor cared. He was no longer cold, but very hot, and he kept trying to ask for water, but no sounds would come from his swollen throat. He had a dream too, a dream of leaving the stifling room for the fresh outer air. His father was in the dream, and so was old Cipactli, only he couldn't see them. He could only hear their voices. After that they were gone and his mother was there. She never left him, and when he muttered or cried out, her soft voice always answered.

When he regained consciousness he realized that it had not been a dream after all. He was at home, in the small room that had been built for the use of the women. The looms had been pushed back against the wall, and he was lying on a pile of soft mats. As he stirred, his mother came forward and bent over him. Her face was drawn, and there were deep shadows encircling her brown eyes, but she was smiling.

"Soon you will be well, Chimal," she said softly. "Your father has given four slaves to be sacrificed, and paid for many feasts. The gods must be satisfied, for now the sores that have covered your body are drying up."

Chimal would have asked her what she meant, but it was too much effort to speak. He closed his eyes and slept.

When he was stronger his mother explained as much to him as she herself could understand. For some unknown reason the gods had become displeased with the boys of the *calmecacs*. Almost every one of them had been afflicted with erupting sores that covered their bodies. A great many already had died from them, despite the efforts of the priests, who worked day and night offering sacrifices to placate the gods.

The sleeping quarters of the students had been turned into a hospital, and Ollin, who had been summoned to pay for a feast after Chimal had fallen ill, had refused to leave his son in the midst of so much suffering. He and Cipactli had wrapped the boy in mats and brought him home for his mother to care for.

"Quauhtli?" demanded Chimal quickly. "Have you

heard of him? He was one of the first to get the red spots."

His mother shook her head. She did not know the names of the other students, and there was nothing more that she could tell him.

"How long have I been here?" he asked.

"Perhaps three weeks. I have not counted the days. You fell ill the night the Spaniards escaped from the city."

"You mean they got away? All of them?" It was hard to believe that the world had been going on without him.

"Many were slain in the attempt. Especially those who had loaded themselves with treasure." She shook her head in disapproval. "The golden chains about their necks weighed them down when they attempted to swim. But Malinche got away, and the traitorous woman whom they call Doña Marina. Your father can tell you about it. He was there. I wasn't."

That evening Ollin told him that the voice of the great drum that had penetrated Chimal's stupor had been sounded by a priest as a signal that the enemy was headed for the causeway of Tlacopan. Immediately every Aztec had taken to his canoe. The three drawbridges crossing the causeway had been destroyed, but the Spaniards had built a portable bridge that they carried with them. As the troops halted while it was being fitted into place, they were besieged by a rain of arrows and rocks from both sides of the lake below.

"It was dark," recalled Ollin, "and Tlaloc was sending the rain. We did not know then that they had brought a bridge with them. We could see only the great dark masses, like thick shadows, and aim as best we could. Finally the shadows began to move, and we continued to send our missiles. When we heard someone cry out, or could see one of the shadows fall, we knew we had found a mark."

It had taken a long time for such a large company to cross the bridge, and then, to their dismay, the Spaniards discovered that the heavy framework had stuck fast to the sides of the dike. It could not be moved to the second opening in the causeway, and the Aztecs found it still in place the following morning. Since there was no turning back, the escaping army continued on to the next break in the causeway. The leading files, urged on by the rear, were crowded together on the brink, then over the edge and into the lake. Here they were on the level with the Aztecs in their canoes, and the carnage was terrible. Some of them managed to swim across, but many more were lost.

"We could use our war clubs," Ollin went on. "And in that way we took many prisoners alive to avenge the honor of the gods."

The opening in the causeway began to fill up with the wreckage of ammunition wagons, heavy guns, chests of solid ingots, bales of rich goods, and bodies of men and horses. Over this passage, those in the rear crossed to the other side.

As they approached the third gap in the causeway the early gray of dawn began to lighten the land. As far as eye could see, the lake was dark with canoes, and the dike was piled with the bodies of the slain. There was nothing for the Spaniards to do at the last break but to plunge over the edge and try to make the opposite side. Some of them succeeded, but many more were lost in this last attempt.

"It was then that I saw Tonatiuh," recalled Ollin,

and his voice held a note of awe. "He is not Quetzal. We all know that. But he must be under the protection of the gods. He was one of the last to attempt the crossing. I saw him fighting on foot, in the midst of a circle of our men. They were using *maquahuitls,* but because his weapon had a longer blade he was able to keep our warriors at a distance. Suddenly he broke through the circle and ran to the edge of the causeway. We all whistled in triumph. We would never have permitted him to swim across, and he knew it."

Chimal couldn't help being a little sorry for Alvarado, who had always been kind to him.

"He picked up a lance," continued Ollin. "Someone must have dropped it there. It was long, very long. Tonatiuh thrust the end of it into the wreckage of the lake. Then, leaning upon it, he seemed to fly through the air. Over he went, and landed safely on the other side! No man could have leaped so far without the help of the gods."

"How many got away?" asked Chimal after a moment.

"I do not know. Perhaps four thousand Tlascalans were slain, and half a hundred Spaniards. And we recovered the bodies of Lord Cacama and two of Montezuma's children who were being taken along as hostages. But Malinche lost the treasure he had stolen from our temples and the royal treasury," concluded Ollin with satisfaction. "His great share, and those of his officers, were strapped on the backs of men of burden. Under the weight, they could not swim the canals, so Malinche leaves the country as poor as he entered it."

This conversation took place on one of the rare, brief visits from his father. During his illness Chimal saw only his mother, for after the rout of the Spaniards every able-bodied man in Tenochtitlán was occupied. The streets had to be cleaned, the drawbridges rebuilt, the market reopened, last honors paid to the warriors who had fallen in battle, and the prisoners they had taken sacrificed to the gods.

The physicians and diviners worked overtime too, for the affliction that had started with the students of the *calmecac* was now being visited on those outside. In their own household Cipactli, the beloved slave, broke out with the red sores one evening, and in an effort to reduce the burning heat that accompanied them he lowered himself from the wharf into the lake. The next morning he was dead.

After that Chimal's mother, who had nursed him patiently through all those weeks, complained of a sore throat and fever. A few hours later the dreaded red bumps appeared on her brown skin, and Chimal, who was now allowed to be up—although his own spots still showed like flat pink blotches and pitted scars—persuaded her to lie down on the mats he had been using. He sent one of the slaves to the market to notify Ollin that more offerings must be made to the gods, this time on Mazatl's account, and he and the maid Tochtli settled down to look after his mother as she had looked after him.

Either they were not as good nurses, or the gods were deaf, for Mazatl, worn out from her long siege of nursing, did not respond. Atototl was sent for from the *ichpochtlaque*, and Ollin stayed home from the market. But by evening of the third day Mazatl was gone.

There was unusual delay in arranging for her funeral. So many were dying of this heretofore unknown affliction that those who had charge of burials could hardly keep up with the demand for their services. It was four days before Mazatl's body, dressed in her best clothes and seated in a low chair, the whole tightly bound in cloth wrappings and decorated with feathers and paper, was carried from the house. Chimal and Atototl watched the departing procession with streaming eyes. Their father accompanied his wife to the part of the city given over to funeral pyres.

"It's all my fault," said Chimal soberly. "The gods meant me to be punished. They only let me go to take her."

Atototl pressed his hand in sympathy, but there was nothing she could say. They both knew this must be the answer.

"I wonder about Quauhtli," continued Chimal. Somehow he felt that he ought to keep talking in an effort to keep his sister's mind from more painful thoughts. "No one here knows about my friends in the *calmecac*. They say that many of them died, but no one knows who."

"Was Quauhtli your special friend?" asked Atototl.

"Yes. We did everything together. His sleeping mat was next to mine, and we always ate together, although we had different classes. And Quauhtli chose me to watch with him from the wall when Malinche returned."

"I'd have liked to see that," Atototl admitted, but without much conviction. "Was it like the time you and Eecatl and I watched from the causeway?"

"Quite a bit." Chimal hesitated, trying to remember the differences. "There were lots more of them this time. And there was a sick man on a litter. I remember that his covering fell off just before they went through the gate. Quauhtli went over the wall and got it."

"What for?"

"As a souvenir. He cut it up and divided with the boys."

"What was his sickness?" asked Atototl. "Was it the red sores?"

Chimal shrugged.

"We didn't see him that close. It could have been."

When Ollin returned the next day he carried a small jar that he buried beneath one of the tiles in the family room.

"Your mother has come home," he told Chimal and Atototl, and they nodded gravely. "We will always honor her memory, and we will try to live our lives in a way that will do her credit."

"What will she want us to do, Father?" Atototl's voice was tearful.

"You are to return to the *ichpochtlaque*. The good women there will continue to instruct you in the arts of womanhood—weaving, embroidery, cooking, and so on."

"But I can do those things already," she protested. "Let me stay home and keep house for you."

"I won't be here." He shook his head. "The emperor Cuitlahua has done me the great honor of requesting my services. I am to be a spy."

"A spy? But you're a trader!" cried Chimal in amazement.

"And what better disguise can a spy assume than that of a wandering trader?" demanded Ollin. "The Spaniards have gone to Tlascala. While traders are not admitted behind their walls, I can go to the border cities, and among the Otomies. Some of them are friendly with the Tlascalans, others with the Aztecs.

I am to keep my eyes and ears open and report anything that seems of value."

"And I suppose I'll have to go back to the *calmecac*," said Chimal hopelessly, thinking how different it would be with so many of his friends gone.

Ollin shook his head.

"The priests of the temple spoke to our emperor about you. They told Cuitlahua that you visited the Palace of Axaya' when the Spaniards were there, and that you learned their language. The reports of the priests were very complimentary about the way you conducted yourself, Chimal." His father smiled proudly. "And the emperor has decided that you shall accompany me to the border cities. Your knowledge of the Spanish tongue may be useful there."

XV

Chimal and his father left the city during the month of Offering of Flowers. When they returned it was the beginning of the month of Severe Weather. From time to time they had sent messengers to the capital with their reports, but now they came themselves, for it was unsafe to remain away any longer. War, like a creeping forest fire, was spreading over the length and breadth of the countryside, and a peaceful trader's caravan was beginning to arouse suspicion.

The Spaniards had reorganized their army. They had received reinforcements from several water-houses that landed on the coast, amounting to over eight hundred men, eighty-seven horses, three large cannon and fifteen smaller ones. What was even worse, they had gained other allies besides the Tlascalans—some by conquest, some by fear and promise of protection. The Tepeacans, the Cholulans, the Itzocans had submitted to the Spanish crown, and a hundred and fifty thousand of their stalwart warriors followed the black velvet standard of Cortés emblazoned with its red cross in flames of blue and white.

Chimal had seen them with his own eyes as they marched out of Tepeaca. He had watched the many-colored plumes of their headdresses floating above the brilliant feathered surcoats, and caught the glint of sunlight on the glassy blades of a sea of *maquahuitls* and copper-headed pikes.

"How can they do it?" he asked his father bitterly. "How can they fight against their own people?"

"Sometimes a man's purse tugs harder than his heartstrings." Ollin sighed. "These vassal cities have resented the annual tribute to Tenochtitlán for a long time."

Day after day their caravan crept along behind the army, seeking to call as little attention to themselves as possible. It was a little past daybreak when they left Tezcuco on the last stage of their journey home. Early as it was, a great crowd of laborers, armed with digging implements, had begun work on a wide trench leading away from the city.

Two Spanish soldiers were directing the work, and Chimal lagged behind the caravan, hoping to pick up a word or two. Although he recognized neither of the overseers as men he had known in the Palace of Axaya', he was glad of his disguise. Every morning he had been careful to smear his face with dirt, and now his body was covered by a long ragged cloak, and instead of the *piochtli* of the schoolboy his hair had been cut one length all over his head.

"It will have to be wider than that," one of the men was saying. "Those brigantines are not canoes, you know."

"It will be," promised the other. "By the time the ships arrive here from Tlascala the canal will be wide enough and deep enough to float them to the lake."

Chimal kept his face expressionless as he turned away to hurry after the others. Once more his knowledge of the Spanish language had proved useful. Now

he knew the answer to a question that had been puzzling his father for weeks.

Although they had not dared venture into Tlascalan territory to see for themselves, Ollin had heard rumors that the Spaniards were building new brigantines to replace those half-completed vessels on the sea coast that Cuitlahua had ordered destroyed. For what purpose they were designed, he had no way of knowing. It seemed unlikely that they were to be used for an attack against Tenochtitlán, for many leagues of dry land lay between Tlascala and the Aztec capital. Nor could they be meant for evacuating the Spaniards from the country, for it was even farther to the sea.

The fragment of conversation told Chimal that the first guess was correct. Canals were being dug that, when filled with water, would bring Spanish ships to the lake enclosing the island city of Tenochtitlán. They could create a blockade even more effective than the one the Aztecs had imposed on the Palace of Axaya'.

Ollin looked grave when he heard what Chimal had to say.

"We must hurry," he decided. "It's only half a league to the beginning of the lake where we keep the canoes. Cuitlahua must have this news at once."

By the time the sun was up, they had come to an open plateau, and before them, unobstructed by wood or hilltop, lay the beautiful valley of Mexico. It was a great basin, guarded by a mountain range of which Old Popo and Iztaccihuatl, the White Woman, the highest peaks, were clothed in eternal snow. The center of the basin was studded with lakes, shimmering like turquoise in the golden sunlight, and clustered about their edges were the rich towns and cities of Iztapalapan, Chalco, Azotzinco, Cuitlahuac, and a dozen others. Some of the lakes were joined by canals, which from this distance looked like ribbons threading them together. But Chimal had eyes only for the largest one, the Tezcucan lake, upon which rose the island capital. That was home! That beautiful jeweled toy held everything that meant the most to him, and he had been gone from it for a very long time.

"Will we see Atototl this evening?" he asked quickly.

"This very evening," promised Ollin, hurrying on. His face seemed brighter, and Chimal realized with a start that in the last few weeks his father had hardly smiled at all.

Traders kept many canoes stationed at different points of the lake, but the man who was in charge of Ollin's was not the one he expected to see.

"Where is Xocotl?" he demanded.

"Xocotl died of the red spots," answered his replacement. Chimal observed that he was only a boy, not even old enough to enter the *telpochcalli.* "When he took sick he sent for me and told me to look after your canoes. My name is Acamapichtli, and I am very good with boats. Xocotl said you would return, and when you did you would pay me. Perhaps you will give me Xocotl's job."

"Of course I will pay you," agreed Ollin. "But as for taking you on permanently, Acama, looking after canoes is a responsible job. It calls for an older man."

"The older men are in the emperor's army," said the boy. "All those who have survived the sickness of the red spots. The emperor Guatemozin needs every warrior."

"Guatemozin!" cried Ollin sharply. "Cuitlahua is the emperor."

"Not since the month of Falling Fruit," corrected

156

Acama. "Cuitlahua served as emperor only four months. Then he died of the red spots just like a common man. Guatemozin is emperor now."

"Then I must see Guatemozin at once," decided Ollin. "Come with us to Tenochtitlán, Acama. You can fasten the canoes together and bring them back. Xocotl's job is yours."

"I thought it would be," agreed Acama cheerfully.

On the way he told them of what had been taking place in Tenochtitlán during their absence. The plague of the red spots had nearly run its course, but not without taking a great toll in lives. Those who had recovered were marked by deep pitted scars, and when he heard this, Chimal nodded. He had a few smallpox scars of his own.

After Cuitlahua had died, and Guatemozin assumed the turquoise crown, he had continued the military plans of his uncle, but with renewed vigor. A beacon fire was laid on every strategic hilltop, which, when kindled, would flare an alarm of the approaching enemy. He had established protective garrisons in all the neighboring cities, and had put a price on the head of any Spaniard brought to Tenochtitlán. The whole city was an armed camp, for the women, children, and the very old, had been sent away to the hills.

"Maybe we won't see Atototl after all," said Chimal when he heard that.

"Probably not," agreed Ollin. "The girls of the school would be among the first to go. But at least we know she's safe."

The new emperor, Acama said, might be found anywhere, for he spent most of the time with his army. But he maintained headquarters in Montezuma's palace, and Ollin decided to seek him there.

"Why don't you go to the *calmecac?*" he suggested to Chimal. "You can visit with your friends while you wait for me."

It was the first time since his illness that Chimal had been back, and the moment he stepped inside the temple gates he felt strange. The buildings were the same. The Great Pyramid still towered above the others, and the wooden shrines that had been burned by the Spaniards had been rebuilt and freshly painted. Incense still curled from the braziers, and the formidable gods stared down as always from their turquoise or amethyst or opal eyes. But there was a feeling of disquietude within the gray walls, and the few students in their white loincloths looked small and young.

A group of them was clustered about the calendar stone, listening to a lecture, and Chimal deliberately went out of his way to pass them. With a start he realized that he knew no one in the class. They were all new students. Moreover, his first impression had been correct. These were no twelve-year-olds. He doubted if they could be more than eight or nine.

He went on to the Temple of Coatlique, his eyes turning this way and that, looking for someone he knew. Since it was afternoon, the grounds should have been swarming with students busy with their daily tasks. All he could see were a few very old priests, and these he recognized only by sight, not by name. One of them was sweeping the pyramid steps, and Chimal went up to him, asking respectfully where he could find the students.

The old priest leaned on his broom and took his time about answering. His wrinkled face bore so many of the pitted scars marking those who had recovered from the sickness that at first Chimal did not recognize him. Then he realized that the priest was Citlalcoatl, who once had been in charge of the health of the students. It was strange that a respected physician-priest should be reduced to sweeping pyramid steps.

"They are gone," answered Citlalcoatl finally, and his voice sounded as far away as his thoughts. "All our fine young men. Our leaders. First the eldest fell in the massacre of the nobles during the Feast of Tlaloc. Then the gods were displeased, and sent a plague—"

"I know," interrupted Chimal quickly. "But they didn't all die from that?"

"No." Citlalcoatl shook his head. "The high priest of Coatlique sent his nephew home to be cared for. I heard that that boy recovered. There were a few others too, whose parents took them away. Some of them may have survived. But the gods were displeased with the *calmecac*. I don't know why. We did our best. The altars ran red with the blood of sacrifice. Until I myself fell victim of the curse I spent every hour brewing medicines and pounding maize for poultices. There was no one to care for me, but somehow the gods did not take me. They let me live."

"There was a boy," interposed Chimal. "He was one of the first to fall ill in the *calmecac* of Coatlique. His name was Quauhtli. Can you tell me about him? Did his parents take him away?"

"He was not Teteoni's nephew?"

"No, no. I am that one."

"You are?" Citlalcoatl looked at him with interest before his eyes grew vague once more. "Then you are very lucky. In Coatlique's *calmecac* you were the only one spared by the gods."

Chimal leaned against one of the carved serpent heads of the banister, and his eyes swam with so many tears that he could no longer see across the square. Quauhtli! His good friend, his laughing, cheerful companion! He couldn't believe it. It must be a mistake.

"You see those boys over there by the calendar stone?" Citlalcoatl's voice droned on in his ear. "Those are the students in the *calmecac* now—in all the *calmecacs* put together. Just one class. Most of them are orphans. Their fathers were lords, killed in battle. But they themselves are too young to fight. They have no place else to go."

Chimal nodded without answering. He sat down on the step, and Citlalcoatl continued with his sweeping. When he finished he turned and spoke kindly to the boy before he left.

"No doubt you have come to see your uncle. You will find him in Coatlique's temple. Last week they brought a young girl here who will impersonate the goddess until the month of Sweeping, when she will be sacrificed. Every day until that time Teteoni must say special prayers and conduct rites to make sure that the maiden will be acceptable to the goddess."

Chimal scarcely heard him. His mind was too filled with grief for Quauhtli and his other friends to think of anything else. How long he sat there on the steps he did not know, but the conical shadows of the pyramids grew long across the paved courtyard and eventually swallowed up the last patch of sunlight.

It was then that the tall figure of a warrior came striding through the outer gate and across the square, straight to the pyramid of Coatlique. Chimal dried his eyes hastily. He didn't want to be caught crying by a soldier.

The stranger was a young man, wearing a tunic stuffed with cotton to ward off arrows. On one shoulder was a shield made of reed and feathers, to designate his rank as captain, and on his head was a wooden helmet trimmed with more feathers and emblazoned with many decorations of gold. He came to a stop before the bottom of the steps, and Chimal cringed, remembering that he was still wearing the ragged cloak of a trader's apprentice and that he had not even stopped to wash the dirt from his face.

"I was told to seek Teteoni, high priest of Coatlique," said the warrior, "but if you are Chimalpopoca, son of Ollin, the trader, my message is for you."

"I am Chimal," he answered faintly, and was relieved to discover that the black eyes fastened upon him were not critical.

"Good." The captain nodded approval. "I am Tlacateotl, one of His Majesty's captains. My message is from Ollin, your father. Guatemozin is very pleased with the reports he brought back concerning the enemy. Ollin has performed a great service for our country, and he has been sent back to see what else he can discover."

"But he can't go without me!" cried Chimal in alarm. He jumped to his feet as though to run after his father.

The captain smiled and put out a hand to stop him.

"It is too late," he said. "He has already gone. This time he went alone. A trader's caravan would be likely to excite suspicion, but a man by himself, particularly one who knows the country, can be very useful."

"But what about me?" asked Chimal. His voice voice quavered, and he didn't even care.

Tlaca hesitated before he spoke.

"Your father has commended you to the care of your uncle Teteoni," he said. "But there was no time to explain to him the present state of our *calmecacs*. Nor did the emperor wish to add to Ollin's worries when he was setting out on this mission. If you wish to stay here, His Majesty will be most agreeable. He is aware of your contribution to Anahuac, and perhaps he can use you further in the ways in which you have been trained."

"Oh," said Chimal weakly.

"But I myself would not care to be a spy," continued Tlaca firmly. "It seems to me that your previous service merits a better reward. You are about twelve years old?"

Chimal nodded. His twelfth birthday had been celebrated at the *calmecac*.

"You have some knowledge of arms?"

"I studied with Ocelotl before I entered the school. There was not too much training here," he added truthfully.

Tlaca frowned.

"I myself was a student at the *calmecac*," he admitted. "I know how much time is wasted in useless studies. Can you handle a canoe?"

"Oh, yes."

"I thought so. The son of a trader would have his own canoe, and be taught how to use it." Tlaca looked at him thoughtfully. "There are many in our army no older than you. They are not used for hand-to-hand combat, but there are other ways in which they can be of service. They can stay with the canoes, run errands, serve as messengers, and fight with *atatls*. If you wish to join my command I will ask His Majesty to give his consent."

Chimal made up his mind instantly. It was not a difficult choice. Life inside the temple walls without Quauhtli and his other friends would be unbearable.

"I'll go with you."

Tlaca promptly lowered himself to the steps.

"You'd better tell your uncle," he suggested. "I'll wait for you here."

Chimal turned and dashed up the stairs as fast as he could go. When he reached the top he saw the high priest prostrated before the stone image of the goddess. He hesitated, reluctant to intrude, and the next moment he felt soft, warm arms holding him fast.

"Chimal! Oh, Chimal. You came! I prayed to the mother of the gods that you would!"

Atototl was clinging to him, laughing and crying at the same time. He put his arm around her awkwardly, staring at her in amazement. It was his sister, but she was different. She had grown taller. Her black hair, which was usually plaited in long braids, fell loose below her waist, and around her head was a circlet of smooth jade stones. She wore a long white gown with a jeweled belt, and on her feet were golden sandals, as fine as those that Montezuma had once owned.

"Atototl," cried Chimal sharply, "what are you doing here, like this?"

Without answering she clung to him more closely, while Teteoni came hurrying from the altar.

"Chimalpopoca! You have come home! Praise to the gods. I will see that they are suitably thanked for their care of you."

"Uncle Teteoni, what is Atototl doing here? Why isn't she in the hills with the others?"

"Atototl has been greatly honored," Teteoni told him gravely. "She has been chosen to be the goddess Coatlique. That is not your sister whom you profane by your touch. It is the goddess herself. She will live here in Tenochtitlán with her people until the month of Sweeping, when she will join the other gods of Anahuac."

Chimal felt Atototl's slight body quiver beneath his arms.

"Take your hands off the goddess!" ordered Teteoni sternly when they continued to stand there.

Chimal obeyed, but not before he had put his mouth against the smooth, dark hair and whispered, "You'll never be sacrificed, Atototl. I'll find a way to save you."

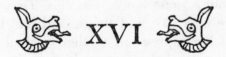

XVI

Chimal had always hated the sacrifices that formed such an important part of the Aztec religion, but never as much as he did now. Always before, the victims had been strangers, prisoners of war and slaves; now the gods had settled upon his own sister, and Chimal was determined that they should never have her. How he was going to bring this about, he did not know. But perhaps Quetzal, who abhorred sacrifice, would show him a way. If he did, Chimal resolved to forsake Huitzil and Tlaloc and all the other bloodthirsty deities of Anahuac and follow only him.

Meanwhile he spent every waking hour learning to be a warrior. Since the emperor Guatemozin had called on every able-bodied man, and it had been years since many of them had held a weapon, there were refresher courses in the use of *maquahuitls*, *atatls*, and bows and arrows. Thanks to Ocelotl's early training, Chimal was able to hold his own, and was soon a member of Tlaca's company.

To his surprise, it was composed of soldiers from the *telpochcalli* at Tlaltelolco, and, to his even greater delight, Eecatl was one of them. But it was not the same as it had been. Eecatl had changed. He had grown tall and broad-shouldered. At thirteen, he was no longer a boy, but a man. He was a seasoned veteran now, and his *piochtli* had been replaced by an *iyac*, which meant that he had taken at least one prisoner.

Chimal's hair was not long enough to cut into a *piochtli*, but no one laughed at this. They all knew of his service as a spy, and they asked him to tell again and again his impressions of their mutual enemy. But his stories were of the past, and when the talks turned to the present, Chimal listened. The soldiers, like the boys of the *calmecac*, had sources that kept them informed of day-by-day events.

The Spaniards had marched from Tezcuco to attack Iztapalapan, which lay on a tongue of land dividing the salt and fresh waters of the great lake. Guatemozin promptly tore down the dikes, and the beautiful garden city was flooded with water. The Spaniards retreated, but the action had an unfortunate effect on some of the other neighboring towns. Otumba and Chalco, both fearing a similar fate, tendered their allegiance to the enemy.

Next the Spanish army, with their ever-increasing horde of allies, reconnoitered the whole of the basin, and Guatemozin sent his armies to help defend the beleaguered towns. It was at Xaltocan that Chimal got his first taste of war, and although he himself did not shoot an arrow, he maneuvered the canoe for those who did.

From the Spanish point of view the campaign was not a great triumph. The inhabitants fled, and although several towns were burned and pillaged, the Aztec forces held their own, capturing many prisoners to carry back to the sacrificial altars at Tenochtitlán.

This was followed by a breathing spell while Cortés withdrew his forces to Tezcuco, where he maintained a permanent camp. Then he attacked once more, this time at Xochimilco, the floating-garden city, less than four leagues from the island capital. Guatemozin immediately dispatched his army to the aid of the considerable forces already there, some on foot, others in a flotilla of canoes. Tlaca's company was among the latter.

"Do you remember the last time we made this trip together?" asked Eecatl. He and Chimal were in the same canoe, and at first Chimal had not been too happy about it. He had become shy around his old friend, who had so far surpassed him as a warrior.

"It was the day the Spaniards came," remembered Chimal. "And you and Atototl and I went to the causeway to see them."

"If we'd only known then what we know now, we'd never have let them in the city." Eecatl shook his head so that the long hair of his *iyac* fell over his right ear.

Chimal regarded it enviously. By this time his own hair had been cut into a stubby *piochtli*, but now the pigtail of the novice had come to feel like a disgrace. He wanted an *iyac*.

"How is Atototl?" asked Eecatl after a moment.

"She's—" Chimal hesitated. In the stir of departure the problem of rescuing his sister had almost faded from his mind. "She's become the goddess Coatlique, in the temple at Tenochtitlán."

Eecatl stared. His mouth dropped open in surprise.

"Atototl? The goddess? Then in the month of Sweeping—"

"She'll be sacrificed." Chimal watched his friend closely. "Unless something happens."

"What could happen?" asked Eecatl after a moment. "It is a great honor to be chosen to be the goddess. It isn't like an ordinary sacrifice."

"You're just as dead afterward," muttered Chimal. He had hoped to find an ally in his old friend, someone to help in Atototl's rescue.

"Don't talk that way!" ordered Eecatl sharply. "Atototl will have a glorious afterlife in the company of the goddess. It is almost better than being a hummingbird with the warriors." As his paddle moved up and down in rhythm with Chimal's his face grew thoughtful. "Perhaps, in this coming battle, we can take care of *your* future."

"What do you mean?"

"You must take a prisoner," Eecatl declared firmly. "It's time you did. I'm tired of looking at your *piochtli*, and you're probably tired of wearing it. I'll help you."

It was night by the time the canoes arrived at the floating gardens of Xochimilco. They tied their craft to small islands and alongside the dike, while they awaited the arrival of their foot soldiers.

Everyone moved quietly, for the Spaniards had taken possession of the town across the causeway. It was built like the other cities in Anahuac, with cottages of clay and light wood, mingled with stone houses of the upper class.

"They will not be able to use their horses here. The streets are too winding," gloated Eecatl. "Remember the first time we saw the horses? We thought they were magic. But on narrow streets and slippery cobblestones they don't count for much."

"Their cannon and harquebuses do," mentioned Chimal.

Guatemozin was learning tactics from the enemy, and he did not wait for daylight to attack. When the signal came to disembark, Eecatl began climbing up the dike.

"Come on," he whispered.

"Tlaca said I was to stay with the canoe," remembered Chimal guiltily.

"No one can see in the darkness. He won't know," insisted Eecatl. "And when you have taken your prisoner, Tlaca will be so proud that he'll forget that you left the canoe."

Desire for an *iyac* outweighed everything else, and Chimal followed his friend up the dike.

In the blackness before pre-dawn, the Aztecs from the canoes joined the marching legions. They swarmed through the town, straight to the temple square where the Spaniards and their allies were encamped. The fighting was hand to hand, *maquahuitls* against Toledo blades, and at first the Aztecs, by virtue of numbers, had the better of it.

Eecatl stayed close to Chimal's side, urging him on, but Chimal needed little urging. In the darkness, which concealed the face of his adversary, it was no harder to do battle in earnest than it had been to perform practice combat under the watchful eye of Ocelotl.

He was engaged with one of the enemy, striking his obsidian-edged *maquahuitl* into the shadows, and trusting to his own senses to know when to parry, when he realized that resistance had ended.

"You got him! He fell!" called Eecatl triumphantly.

Chimal's eyes strained into the knot of shadows before him. It was much closer to the ground than it had been a moment before.

"He dropped his sword."

"Then grab him." Eecatl sprang forward to help, and Chimal groped after the retreating adversary, who was attempting to crawl away. His hand closed around an arm encased in thick, padded cotton, and at the same moment his ears throbbed to the roar of musketry. About them rained a sudden sea of arrows as the Spanish crossbowmen finally assembled and let forth a stream of fire.

"You've taken one alive!" Eecatl's voice shrilled loud above the tumult. "Get him to the canoe. I'll help you tie him."

Dragging the protesting captive between them, they joined the retreating Aztecs, who had long since learned to take cover in the face of gunfire. Down one of the narrow, crooked streets they ran, and in the protection of a doorway stopped to secure their prisoner. Eecatl trussed the man's arms tight to his body with a length of rope, leaving his feet free so that he could walk. Then he gave the end of the rope to Chimal.

"Better take him down and put him in one of the smaller canoes," he advised. "And then, if I were you, I'd start back for Tenochtitlán with him."

"And leave the fighting?" Chimal gasped.

"We don't take many prisoners alive," Eecatl reminded him ruefully. "They'd rather fight to the death than be sacrificed. The priests will be pleased to get this one, and Tlaca would rather you deliver him than stay. It will just be skirmishes from now on, anyway."

Chimal nodded and jerked on the rope. His prisoner tried to resist, stumbled, then finally followed after.

"And you earned your *iyac!*" called Eecatl joyfully.

Chimal smiled to himself. How wonderful it would be to lose the despised pigtail. How proud Ollin would be when he returned! And Atototl— But it was better not to think of Atototl at a time like this.

Getting his prisoner down the dike singlehanded

presented difficulties. With his bound hands, the man could not help himself, and Chimal was afraid to untie him. Finally he pushed the resisting captive off the causeway, and as soon as he heard the splash, he himself dived in and recovered the kicking, sputtering figure.

It was almost as hard to get him into one of the canoes, but this time the prisoner did not try to hold back. He let himself go limp, and through chattering teeth he kept muttering, "Holy Mother, help me. Help me!"

A Spaniard! Chimal recognized in surprise. By the padded coat sleeve, he had taken his captive for a Tlascalan. This was even a greater prize than he had imagined.

Dawn was dissolving the blackness by the time the Spaniard lay stretched out in the canoe and Chimal picked up his paddles. Behind and above him the sounds of battle continued from the causeway and from the city of Xochimilco. He felt a little like a deserter as he maneuvered his way through the maze of islands leading to the canal, but Eecatl had told him to go, and Eecatl was experienced in these things.

He glanced triumphantly at his prisoner, now lying quietly in the bottom of the canoe, and saw that he himself was being observed in turn. Then he looked again. The white face under the long, streaming reddish-brown hair was familiar. It was Orteguilla, the page.

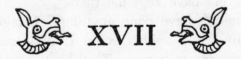

XVII

"Orteguilla!" Chimal gasped.

"Hello, Chimal." The page smiled faintly. "I didn't know it was you."

"Nor I you."

"Would it have made any difference?" asked Orteguilla quickly.

Chimal reminded himself that this was the enemy. He thought of the massacre of the nobles, and of all the brave men of Anahuac who had given their lives since the Spaniards came. He remembered how the temples had been desecrated and the treasure stolen, and that Malinche and his own people were now at war. He shook his head so vigorously that the *piochtli* bounced against his shoulders.

"No."

"I suppose it couldn't." Orteguilla sighed. "I suppose this was bound to happen sometime. I was never very good with a sword. I'm used as a messenger, not a soldier. But your attack this morning was a surprise. So long as I had to be taken by someone, I'm glad it was you."

"Why?" Chimal frowned deeply, and pretended to be very busy with his paddling.

"Because I wanted to see you again. I wanted to tell you about the day when your nobles were killed. I wanted you to know I'm sorry. I don't think it was chivalrous. I didn't think so then, and I still don't."

"You should have warned me," accused Chimal. "You shouldn't have kept me there."

"You couldn't have done anything," Orteguilla told him wearily. "And neither could I. Besides, I wasn't sure it was going to happen. They kept it pretty quiet. I'd heard a rumor, but I wasn't sure it was true. And I couldn't ask. They wouldn't have told me."

"I suppose not," agreed Chimal after a moment. It helped a little to know that Orteguilla hadn't deliberately conspired against him.

"I was afraid it was true, though," confessed Orteguilla. "And I was afraid you might be hurt. That's why I kept you there as long as I did that afternoon. I think that Don Pedro felt like that too. It was his idea that we have the party."

Chimal's forgiveness could not extend to the golden-haired Tonatiuh. After all, he had known what was going to happen. He had planned it.

"Where are you taking me?" asked the page after a long silence.

"To the temple. To Tenochtitlán."

"I'm going to be sacrificed?" Orteguilla's voice was sharp with horror.

Chimal nodded, trying not to think of what was going to happen.

"How can you do that?" cried Orteguilla. "We were friends. You'll have my blood on your conscience, and God will never forgive you."

Chimal avoided the last of the islands, turning his canoe into the still waters of the canal. But Orteguilla's words made him uncomfortable. It was true that

Huitzil and Tlaloc and the lesser deities would rejoice, but what would Quetzal think?

"Does it hurt much?" asked the page in a small voice.

"I don't know. It's over soon." Chimal tried to be as consoling as he could. Waiting would be the hardest, knowing that eventually you must climb those three flights to the pyramid's top, and that you'd never come down. That was the agony which Atototl was enduring right now. It would go on for her until the month of Sweeping, unless Chimal could find a way to save her.

And then, as clearly as though it was the voice of Quetzal speaking to him, he knew what he must do.

"Orteguilla," he said quickly, "if I save you, if I don't turn you over to the priests, but help you get back to your own people, will you do something for me?"

"Anything!" The page struggled to sit up, found it was impossible, and lay back down.

"Will you take my sister to Doña Marina? Will you ask her to look after Atototl as though she were her own daughter, and keep her from harm?"

"Of course. But I don't understand."

"You don't have to. Not now," declared Chimal. "I don't know how I'm going to do it. Getting Atototl out of the temple will be the hardest. But there has to be a way. Quetzal will help me."

"And the Holy Mother will help me," added Orteguilla. "She already has."

It was late afternoon when Chimal tied his canoe to the landing beside the Great Temple at Tenochtitlán. There had been no sleep on the night before, and no time to rest during the day, but he did not feel tired. Excitement was keeping him going. If his plan was to

175

succeed, it had to be executed now, for a white-skinned boy could not long be kept hidden in a city of brown-skinned people.

He had left Orteguilla in one of his father's warehouses at Tlaltelolco, and although only Tochtli was at home, getting him into the warehouse had not been easy. Orteguilla had remained hidden in the bottom of the canoe, while Chimal sent the maid scurrying about on errands. When he was sure that she was out of sight he cut the ropes tying the page and whisked him into the empty warehouse. Before slamming the door, he tossed in one of Tecpatl's cloaks, which had been freshly washed and hung to dry in the sun. Orteguilla could wrap himself in the garment when it was time to leave.

It took a little while to collect the various items that he needed, and then, because Tochtli had prepared food, he thought it best to eat. She might have found it strange had he refused.

As he paddled down the canal toward Tenochtitlán he wondered how the battle was going at Xochimilco, and how he could explain to Eecatl how he had come to lose his prisioner. Perhaps it would be best to say that it had happened when he pushed the man off the dike.

The courtyard of the temple was as he had seen it on his last visit, except that no class in reckoning was being held around the calendar stone. He carried the bulky bundle, that he had brought from home to the sleeping quarters of Coatlique's *calmecac*. The diminished group of students was obviously using another dormitory, and Chimal doubted if anything left there would be discovered immediately. When he came back outside, he carried only a slim golden flask concealed beneath the folds of his cloak.

He glanced up to the top of the pyramid towering above the low buildings occupied by the school, and caught his breath in delight. It was as if Quetzal were helping him, making things easy. Three persons were descending the stairs from the temple. Two wore the long black robes of Coatlique's priestesses, but the third was gowned in white. Long black hair fell down her back to below her waist.

Chimal hurried to the bottom of the steps, and as soon as the group reached the last flight he called to his sister. Immediately the two priestesses, who had been following respectfully behind, rushed ahead, their arms thrust out in protection of their charge.

"It's all right," Chimal assured them. "I mean no harm. I'm Chimalpopoca, nephew of Teteoni. I just want to speak to my sister, Atototl."

"There is no person named Atototl here!" cried one of the priestesses. Her voice was sharp, and she continued to hold out her arms, preventing the girl behind from continuing on down the steps.

Both the women were old, Chimal observed, but they were not feeble. They were prepared to defend themselves and the white-robed Atototl. What was worse, they could call out for help, and then he might never have a chance to talk with his sister alone.

"Who is that behind you?" he asked cautiously.

"This is the goddess Coatlique," answered the priestess, "mother of the sun, moon, and stars, mother of Huitzil, Lady of the Skirt of Serpents. She is no mortal woman, and no sister of yours. Be on your way."

"I am Coatlique, Lady of the Skirt of Serpents." Atototl's voice spoke coldly from behind her black-robed guardians. Her dark eyes looked out over the courtyard, ignoring her brother at the bottom of the

178

steps. "I am mother of the sun, the moon and stars, and of Huitzil, god of the blue sky and of war, patron of Tenochtitlán. So that my remaining days in the city of my son shall be happy, it is the duty of those who serve me to grant my every wish."

"So it shall be, my lady!" cried both priestesses, turning to look at her.

"It is my wish to speak with this mortal in private," announced Atototl icily. "Go, both of you. Wait at a distance."

Although they obeyed without protest, Chimal could see that the old women were not pleased. Their faces, as they passed him, were set with disapproval. They huddled at the foot of the stairs, whispering together and glaring the hatred at him that they did not dare vent against one who impersonated their goddess.

Chimal climbed to the place where Atototl stood waiting. She did not look at him, but kept her eyes fastened on the Great Pyramid in the center of the square. Her lips barely moved with her whispered words.

"I knew you'd come, Chimal. How are you going to get me away? And where can we go that Uncle Teteoni won't find us?"

"A friend of mine is going to hide you," answered Chimal. There was no time to go into the matter of Orteguilla and Doña Marina now. "But I don't know how I'm going to get you away from here. Not entirely. I did bring a disguise, the skirt and blouse of a serving girl, and a dark shawl to cover your head. I left them in the sleeping quarters of the *calmecac*."

Although Atototl kept the rest of her face expressionless, her eyes began to sparkle.

"And I brought some of Father's cactus wine," continued Chimal. "It's very strong. I thought it might be useful. Outside of that, I haven't any plan."

"The two black vultures who guard me day and night love wine!" For the first time Atototl looked at him directly. Her eyes were dancing. "Where is it?"

The flask changed places from beneath Chimal's cloak to the folds of Atototl's white robe.

"You have a boat?"

"Tied up to the temple wharf."

"Wait in it. I will come there during the night," she promised. Then, raising her voice, she ordered. "Go away, young warrior. The girl you seek is no more, and the goddess Coatlique has more important matters to concern her mind than you."

She swept past him down the stairs, and when she reached the bottom the old priestesses crowded close on either side. Together they disappeared into the doorway that led to their apartments.

When they had gone Chimal returned to his canoe. Those hours of waiting were the longest he had ever spent. While it was still daylight he was sure that the people in the street and in boats on the canal were staring at him, wondering why he, in the dress of a warrior, was not off helping the others at Xochimilco. Perhaps they thought he was afraid, and that was why he still wore the *piochtli* of the novice. It was a relief when darkness followed the sunset, but then it began to grow cold, and while his padded jacket kept his body warm, his feet grew numb and icy.

He saw the beacon fires on the surrounding hills open like orange and crimson flowers in the gathering dusk. He heard the priests from the temple call the hours, and heard the throaty voices of their conch shells. A million stars overhead stared down accusingly, but Chimal tried not to think of them, for every star was a god and knew that he was here to deprive their mother, the goddess Coatlique, of her chosen sacrifice.

It was long after midnight when Atototl joined him, and Chimal had almost given her up. Her bare feet made no noise on the smooth stones, and the dark garments blended into the shadows so that he did not even see her coming.

"Give me an oar," she ordered, lifting her long skirts to step into the canoe. "We'll make better time if we both paddle. Where are we going?"

"Home first." Chimal pushed off against the wharf into the darkness. *Thank you, Quetzal,* he said silently. *And please don't leave us now.*

Because sound carries over water, they talked little on the way and then only in whispers.

"Did you have trouble getting away?" Chimal had to know.

"No." He heard Atototl smother a giggle. "It was fun. I told the priestesses the wine was sent by the gods as a reward for their good service. You should have seen them swallow it down. They were both snoring when I left."

One other thing Chimal had to tell her before they picked up Orteguilla. "My friend, the boy who is taking you to the hiding place, is a Spaniard."

"A Spaniard!"

"Shh. Yes. He's very nice. He will be good to you. And the woman to whom he is taking you will be kind too. She owes a debt to Father. I don't know any place else where you'll be safe."

Atototl did not answer. But at least she was prepared for Orteguilla when Chimal brought him from the warehouse to the canoe. Her black eyes watched the

Spanish boy curiously as he climbed in to lie on the floor between them. Then, when Chimal nodded toward the opposite shore, she picked up her paddle, still without speaking.

By this time it was growing light enough to see. When they turned out of the canal and onto the lake Atototl decided that it was safe to ask questions.

"Where is this woman to whom your friend is taking me?"

"She's with the Spaniards. With Malinche." Chimal tried to make his voice matter-of-fact.

Atototl stopped paddling immediately. She turned around, facing her brother.

"I won't go," she declared. "You should have told me

before. I'd rather be sacrificed as Coatlique than eaten by Spaniards."

"Eaten by Spaniards?" Orteguilla sat up, throwing off the white cloak that had covered him. He spoke enough of the Aztec tongue to understand the last three words. "What are you talking about? We don't eat people!"

"Lie down, Orteguilla!" cried Chimal in alarm. "What if someone should see you?"

But Orteguilla wouldn't lie down. He sat upright, glaring at Atototl, who returned his stare appraisingly.

"Spaniards—do—not—eat—people," repeated Orteguilla, speaking very slowly.

Atototl believed him.

"Oh," she said in a mollified tone. "I was afraid they might. All right, then. I'll go with you."

She turned back to pick up her stroke, Orteguilla lay down in the canoe, and Chimal breathed a sigh of relief. His sister's curiosity would keep her on her way until she reached Doña Marina, and after that he would have to trust the Aztec woman to keep Atototl contented.

As they neared the center of the lake Chimal could see across to the opposite shore. When they had set out, an early fog had clouded his distant view, but now he could perceive that the whole beach had undergone a change. Some of the wharfs were still there, but the mouth of an inland channel now opened up into the lake, and the shore beside it was crowded with men. As he stared, he caught the glint of the rising sun on armor, and saw the jagged outline of the animal head-dresses worn by the Tlascalans.

"Orteguilla, sit up!" he ordered tersely.

The page threw off the cloak and obeyed. His eyes

brightened as they fastened on the opposite shore, and he began to count rapidly on his fingers.

"Yes," he declared. "This is the day. They're on schedule."

"The day for what?"

"The day they're launching the brigantines—thirteen of them. Lieutenant Sandoval brought them overland on the backs of porters from Tlascala, and they were reassembled at Tezcuco. There's a channel dug from there to the lake, and when they're launched they'll set up a blockade around Tenochtitlán that no one can get through. We got out just in time."

Chimal's heart soared into his throat, and he could hear it fluttering in his ears. This was the very thing that his father had feared might happen. He wondered what Guatemozin would do about it. The new emperor had an answer for most of the enemy's plans. Chimal must hurry back to warn him, but first he had to land Atototl where she would be safe.

Orteguilla began to wave as they approached the shore, and after a minute a few hands returned his salute. Chimal paddled stolidly on. When they were close he jumped out and pulled the canoe up on the beach. All around him he could hear voices welcoming the page, demanding to know where he had been, and what he was doing in the company of two Aztecs.

Chimal gave his hand to Atototl, and for a moment they stood there forgotten. The Tlascalans eyed them insolently, and Chimal squeezed his sister's fingers. Then Orteguilla broke loose from the group of well-wishers.

"We'll go straight to Tezcuco," he announced happily. "Doña Marina is there, although Cortés is still at

184

Xochimilco. She may join him later when he's captured that town and moves on to the next."

Chimal turned to his sister.

"Go with him, Atototl," he ordered.

"We'll all go," insisted Orteguilla quickly. "Surely you won't try to go back now, Chimal. This is the beginning of the end."

"I must go," said Chimal.

Amid the jeers of the Tlascalans, he turned and walked back to his canoe.

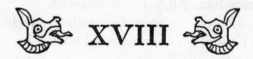

XVIII

Almost immediately the residents of Tenochtitlán began to feel the effects of the Spanish blockade. Simultaneously with the launching of the brigantines on the lake Cortés divided his forces, swollen by the armies of subjugated towns, and soon he held all the causeways leading to the city. It was no longer possible for the Aztecs to bring fresh produce from the inland farms to the market of Tlaltelolco.

One by one the domestic animals, largely family pets, turkeys, rabbits, and hairless dogs, disappeared into stewpots, but what was even more alarming was the shortage of drinking water. The Spaniards cut off the pipes that carried the main supply of water over high aqueducts from Chapultepec. Now there remained only the few fresh springs scattered throughout the city, for the lake itself was salt.

Chimal had rejoined his company as soon as he could after leaving Orteguilla and Atototl, and to his relief he found that he had not been missed. The Aztecs, defeated at Xochimilco, had retreated, fighting, to Cojohuacan, which likewise fell. Companies were scattered and could not be reassembled until they were back in Tenochtitlán. No one asked where he had been.

Eecatl was disappointed to hear that Chimal had lost his prisoner, but not surprised.

"It's my fault," he conceded generously. "I should have helped you over the dike. But there's still time. We'll get you that *iyac* yet."

Chimal felt guilty at deceiving his friend, but Eecatl would never understand the necessity of saving Atototl.

The assignment given to Tlaca's men was to harry the brigantines that patrolled the lake. Guatemozin was too smart a general to engage the Spanish navy in actual combat. The vessels were armed with cannon, for which he had learned a healthy respect. But he soon learned that the great sails would not fill unless a wind swept across the water, and at such times they must remain motionless.

Under cover of darkness Chimal and the others drove pilings into the shallows of the southern side of the lake. When morning came their canoes lay in ambuscade among the tall reeds that fringed the shore. Later several larger boats were sent out on the lake as decoys, and the Spaniards, supposing them to be running the blockade for provisions, set out in pursuit. When the Aztec boats fled for shelter to the reedy banks the Spaniards followed and were soon entangled by the palisades and overwhelmed by the enemy.

This happened not once but several times. Moreover, on windless nights Tlaca's men were sometimes able to steal across the lake and bring needed provisions for the crowded population now gathered in the city.

Eventually this came to an end. One after another the great towns about the lake cast off their allegiance to Tenochtitlán. Xochimilco, Cojohuacan, Tacuba swore their allegiance to the Spanish throne and sent their remaining warriors to follow the standard of Cortés. The captains of the brigantines grew familiar with the ambushes next to shore and refused to fall into the trap.

There was nothing to do but sit day after day watching the brigantines that swept the lake and speculating on the fighting that was going on without them. Isolated as they were, they had no way of knowing what was happening only a few miles distant.

Eventually Tlaca sent a messenger to Guatemozin, acquainting him with this state of affairs and suggesting that his men would be more useful elsewhere. His request was denied.

"Somebody has to defend the shore," reasoned Chimal when they heard the decision. "We can't just leave it for the enemy."

"But why does it have to be *our* company?" fumed Eecatl. "The real fighting's going on in the city. You can hear the guns from here."

"I know." Chimal nodded. He wondered how much of the city would remain by the time they were relieved. Every night the sky was red from the fires started by the Spaniards. One terrible evening they watched in awed silence as great sheets of flame shot up above the temple square. Even the gods were not safe from the torches of the enemy.

The weeks slid by into months, and still Guatemozin kept insisting that their small company stay where it was.

"We are only twenty men," repeated the messenger returning with the emperor's reply to Tlaca's second request to be relieved. "Twenty men mean little in an army of many thousands, but they might mean much in defense of our shore line. If Malinche lifts the blockade, or if he moves to land, we are to send word immediately."

"A few of those twenty men might be able to give a pretty good account of themselves in battle if they had a chance," growled Eecatl. "And besides, we're getting a little tired of eating nothing but fish."

During the months of Drought, of Bean Porridge, and of the Feasts of the Lesser and Greater Lords, Tlaca's company continued to stand guard along the shore, catching and eating fish from the lake and fuming about their assignment. But with the month of Offering of Flowers those who went out on the lake for food returned with only small catches that grew smaller each day. When it got to the point where one or two small fish, boiled into broth, provided sustenance for the whole company in a single day, Tlaca took things into his own hands.

"Our last two messengers have not returned, but the emperor wouldn't want us to starve," he decided. "We'll go to the city, where we can get something to eat. If he sends us back, we'll come—but not before we've had a chance to fill our stomachs and see what is going on."

They started up the nearest canal leading from the lake to the Great Temple at Tenochtitlán, and the farther they advanced, the greater grew their uneasiness.

At the beginning there were only a few small scattered fishing huts set in the reedy swamps, but every one seemed to be deserted. Not a man, or woman, or child was to be seen, and theirs were the only canoes in the waterway. As they approached what had been the outskirts of the city the canal ended. It was filled up with rocks and stones, the debris of former dwellings. These had been razed to the ground, their roofs and interiors burned, and the charred timbers thrown into the channel, leveling it to the height of the ground around. No grass grew in the empty courtyards; they were dug up and furrowed as though turned over for a planting, and the bushes were stripped of leaves, so that they looked like thin brown sticks.

"Leave the canoes!" ordered Tlaca. "We go on foot."

The farther they penetrated the city, the more unrecognizable it became. What had been a beautiful, sparkling metropolis had disappeared. Trees had been chopped to the ground, as much of the houses as were built of wood had been burned, and the charred timbers, with the fresh logs and branches, and the stones and plaster from the exteriors had been thrown into the canal, blocking the water and leveling everything to a barren wasteland.

When they reached the temple square they could see the results of those flames that had flooded the sky a few weeks ago, and the sight was far worse than any of them had imagined. Here the fighting must have been desperate indeed. The enemy had thrown torches and firebrands so that the palaces of Axaya' and Montezuma, as well as the temples atop the many pyramids, were but stone shells filled with charcoal and ashes. The interiors, the turrets, the roofs, everything built of wood was now destroyed. And once again the stone idols had been rolled down the stairs, this time to help choke the canals.

"Where is everyone? Where are the priests?" whispered Chimal, thinking of his uncle Teteoni.

"I don't know." Eecatl shook his head. "What could have happened while we were sitting on the lake? How could we have not known this was going on?"

Tlaca, his face grave and worried, came to a decision. "We'll march down one of the avenues a way," he said. "There must be someone left who can answer our questions."

They stayed close together, *maquahuitls* in hand, looking from side to side. In the gutters lay the unburied dead. Some of them were Aztecs, which was even more alarming, since ceremonial burial was a rite performed after every battle. Streets were blocked with stones thrown down by defenders on rooftops, and the residential sections had been burned and razed like the temples.

"There's someone!" cried Tlaca, who was leading the way. He rushed ahead, his company close on his heels.

An old man was digging up shoots of grass from between the cobblestones. He saw them and straightened up, awaiting their arrival.

"Where is everyone?" cried Tlaca. "Where's Guatemozin and his army?"

"The others have gone to Tlaltelolco," quavered the old man. "It is easier to defend one place than a whole city. But I stayed behind. Malinche will not come seeking one man. I was right too." He nodded craftily. "For three days I have heard the sounds of their thunder weapons from that direction."

"Well, at least Guatemozin will have the market at Tlaltelolco," mused Tlaca. "It is easier to fight on a full stomach."

The old man shook his head.

"The market has been empty for weeks. They're eating grass and algae from the lake there, just as we were here."

"Set out at once!" ordered Tlaca quickly.

Now that the waterways throughout the city had been converted to dry land it took some time to reach their destination, but on the flat plateau, unobstructed by buildings and trees, they could see for miles ahead. Darkness was on them by the time they reached the outskirts of the suburb, but before that happened they had witnessed, across the wasteland, the enemy retreating across the giant western causeway. From this distance the Spaniards looked like tiny dolls parading across a miniature bridge. First came the cavalry, then the foot soldiers, and finally their Indian allies. There were thousands upon thousands of these.

"They're retreating!" cried Chimal hopefully. "Were they—do you think—"

"No," said Eecatl shortly. "They're just leaving for the night. You don't see Guatemozin's troops pursuing, do you?"

As they entered Tlaltelolco, the last stronghold of the Aztecs, Chimal could hardly keep from crying. Every bit of ground had been torn up in the search for roots and stems; the trees were stripped of leaves and bark; and although in this place there were living men, they had been too busy with defense or too weak from hunger to bury the dead. Already the canal was filling with timbers and rocks from the razed buildings, and a level area, well suited for battle, was beginning to encroach into the suburb.

Once they arrived, Tlaca made no effort to keep his company together. These were Tlaltelolcoan men, and none would be content until he had sought out his own home.

"Before daylight," he said simply. "Meet at the *telpochcalli*."

Chimal struck out alone through the darkness. It took nearly an hour to reach the district where the merchants and traders lived, for the streets were so filled with people wandering aimlessly that they held him back.

The gate leading to the house of Ollin was closed tight, and Chimal pounded for a long time before anyone answered. Finally a voice came through the heavy boards, ordering him to go away.

"We're all filled up! There's no more room."

"But I'm Chimal!" he called desperately. "Chimal-popoca, son of Ollin. I live here. This is my house."

"What was your mother's name? And your sister's?" The muffled voice was sharp with surprise, but still suspicious.

"My mother was Mazatl, and Atototl is my sister. And you are Tecpatl," he answered impatiently, conscious that a crowd was gathering about him, listening to the conversation.

"Stand close to the gate!" ordered Tecpatl. "Be ready when I open."

There was the scrape of the wooden bar being raised; then the gate swung open a small crack. Chimal found himself being pushed forward and inside, as the crowd tried to follow him through. Tecpatl was ready for them, and even with his single arm managed to slam the gate shut behind the boy.

"Why did you ask all those questions?" demanded Chimal angrily.

"Others would have entered if they could. There was no room." Ollin's most trusted retainer shrugged. "I had to make sure that it was you. Welcome, Chimal. We feared, your father and I, that you were dead."

Two torches cast a flickering light over part of the courtyard before them, and Chimal stared in amazement. Every available foot of space was occupied by a

193

sleeping man. They lay side by side, head to foot, extending into the shadows beyond the torchlight.

"These are warriors," explained Tecpatl. "They must have a place to rest or they cannot rise to fight tomorrow. That is why we must keep the others out."

"And do you feed them too?" Chimal gasped.

"No. We have no food. That they must find for themselves," Tecpatl told him. "I do not know how they manage. As for us, Tochtli and I spend the day gathering the green growth from the top of the lake. She dries it into cakes for your father and us. It is not enough, but it keeps us alive."

"My father is here?" cried Chimal joyfully.

Tecpatl smiled and nodded. He motioned Chimal to follow him into the house.

As they passed open doorways the boy could see that every room was filled with sleeping warriors. Only the small workroom that had once been his mother's was reserved for the use of the family, and here Ollin lay on a bed of mats.

"Chimal! My son!" Ollin tried to sit up but fell back, and Chimal saw that he was swathed in bandages.

"You're hurt!" he cried in alarm.

"I will live." His father smiled. "Thanks to my friend Tecpatl."

"Give thanks instead to the bounty of the gods!" The sharp correction came from the shadows beyond the light cast by the indoor torch, and for the first time Chimal was aware of the presence of his uncle. The high priest sat cross-legged on a floor mat, and his black robes and long matted hair that fell about his face made him almost invisible.

"Greetings, reverend uncle," said Chimal cour-

teously. "I worried about you after seeing what had happened to the Great Temple."

There will be a day of retribution," claimed Teteoni darkly. "The gods of Anahuac but await the moment of their own choosing before they strike down these false strangers."

"Pray that the day comes soon before all our people are destroyed," said Ollin. His voice was weak, but Chimal sensed a faint note of criticism.

"Tell me how you were hurt," he begged quickly. "I thought you had gone away, and were serving as a spy for the emperor."

"When the enemy is in your own city there is no need to spy on him elsewhere," said Ollin sadly. "When I returned I took my place with the warriors. I was in the battle of the Great Temple, where I fell before the *maquahuitl* of a Tlascalan. He left me for dead, and I lay there for almost two days. Then Tecpatl came, searching the field for my body. With his one arm he carried me home, and he and Tochtli have cared for me ever since. But tell me of yourself. Where have you been?"

"With Tlaca's company," answered Chimal briefly. "Spying on the brigantines. Our last two messengers to Guatemozin, begging for relief from that duty, did not return, and we did not know until today what was going on in the city."

"Then you do not know about the great honor that has been bestowed upon this family by the gods?" Teteoni lifted his head, and the pale circle of his face glimmered faintly in the shadows.

"Honor? What honor?"

"A great honor. I have never heard its like before." Teteoni spoke proudly. For a moment the desecration of the temple was forgotten. "It was to your former sister, she who had become the living reincarnation of the goddess Coatlique."

"To Atototl?" Chimal's heart began to pound. He had thought her safe with Doña Marina and Orteguilla. Could it be possible that she had been captured?

"One night the goddess herself appeared before the two priestesses who were in charge of your former sister," explained Teteoni with relish. "She told them that she had come to take her incarnation away from an earth filled with violence. She left behind, as proof of having been here, a rich flask that had been used for holy wine, and she spirited the girl away."

In his relief, Chimal began to laugh. Obviously the two priestesses had concocted the story to escape punishment for letting their charge escape. The more he thought about it, the funnier it became.

"Why do you find it so amusing?" Ollin's voice was reproachful, and Chimal made an effort to stifle his mirth.

"Your laughter offends the gods," declared Teteoni. Then he added severely to Ollin, "But no more than your tears. You should rejoice that a child of yours has found favor with those most high."

"I do," agreed Ollin, wiping his eyes. "But I also grieve that I shall never see her again. Atototl was dear to me."

Hunger had made Chimal lightheaded, and he had walked many miles since daybreak. He was so tired that he could hardly think, and now the only thing that seemed important was to reassure his father.

"But you *will* see her again!" he cried recklessly. "Just as soon as the war is over. It wasn't the goddess who took Atototl away. It was I. She's in a safe place where no one will harm her."

"But the priestesses said it was the goddess!" Teteoni stood up. The torchlight shining on his lined face made it terrible to see. "And she left wine."

"The priestesses lied," declared Chimal bravely. "And the wine came from my father's warehouse."

"You have cheated the gods!" shrilled Teteoni angrily. "You have made mockery of their priests. There is only one way to atone. Your blood must flow on their altars."

"No!" cried Ollin, attempting to rise.

At the same moment Chimal felt himself grasped round the shoulders by Tecpatl's arm and propelled violently from the room. He was hurried through the ranks of snoring warriors, away from the torchlight and into the shadowy depths toward the lake.

"Get in the canoe," whispered Tecpatl softly as they stepped onto the wharf. "You can sleep there until morning."

"What then?" asked Chimal fearfully. The dullness had dissolved from around his brain, and he was well aware of the consequences that must follow his confession.

"Leave with the warriors," advised Tecpatl. "In the crowd you will not be noticed. Your father and I will try to reason with Teteoni. I am sure he will not come seeking you tonight. Perhaps we can persuade him to keep the secret."

Chimal nodded unhappily as he climbed into the canoe. Nothing, he was sure, would dissuade the high priest from his resolve.

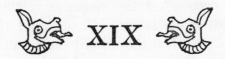 XIX

Before daylight the soldiers had all gone, and Chimal left with them. Tecpatl, who held open the gate so that the men could file through, caught at Chimal's arm as he went by.

"Your uncle has gone back to the temple," he said in a low voice. "He would promise nothing."

Chimal nodded miserably. He had known all along that the high priest could not be sworn to silence.

"I will hang a white cloth from the rooftop whenever he or anyone from the temple is here," promised Tecpatl hurriedly. "Watch for it before you enter at night. And be careful. You are only a boy. Your father and I are worried about you."

Although the warriors waited until after sunup, the Spaniards did not return. Finally the Aztecs received word that Cortés had called a two-day truce. He had sent an emissary laying down terms of surrender to Guatemozin, for he did not want to continue the destruction of the city. He had given the emperor forty-eight hours to consider the proposal and make up his mind.

On hearing this, the warriors scattered, each in pursuit of something to put in his stomach. There were rats and lizards to be caught, and an occasional songbird might be brought down by an arrow. Chimal returned home, and when he saw that there was no white cloth hanging from the roof he went inside. It was his duty to help Tecpatl and Tochtli search for food.

On the evening of the second day they received another visit from Teteoni. Chimal had been sitting with his father when they heard the pounding on the gate. He left the room and circled the outside of the building. In the back was an open window through which he could listen unobserved.

Tecpatl made a great deal of noise, ushering Teteoni into Ollin's presence. He stumbled over the sleeping men in the courtyard and spoke in a loud voice, several times calling the high priest by name. Chimal smiled to himself in the darkness. Tecpatl was a loyal friend.

Ollin greeted his brother-in-law courteously but with a certain reserve.

"How can I serve you?" he asked.

"You can offer me hospitality, if you have it." Teteoni's voice came floating through the window, and Chimal could picture his uncle settling himself on one of the floor mats. "Food is scarce at the temple."

"It is scarce everywhere," said Ollin. "Give him an algae cake, Tecpatl. It is all we have."

Chimal writhed in indignation. He himself had helped gather the mucilaginous substance that made those cakes. It was found floating on the lake, but in such small quantities that it took a long time to collect. Dried and baked by Tochtli, it tasted a little like cheese, and it was all they had eaten for two days. He resented the fact that his uncle, who probably enjoyed a better diet at the temple, was taking some of their food.

"Where is Chimalpopoca?" demanded Teteoni after a short interval of chewing.

"He has gone away," said Ollin. He hesitated, then asked, "Have you told the other priests about Chimal?"

"I am the servant of the gods, and it was my duty to tell. I am fond of Chimal, but he has sinned, and he alone can atone for those sins. No other sacrifice will do this time."

Ollin and Tecpatl were silent, and after a moment Teteoni continued.

"I know that he is here, and I have come to fetch him. The Lady of the Skirt of Serpents will look upon him more kindly if he goes willingly. If not, we will find him."

Chimal's heart pounded so loudly that he was afraid it would betray him. The other night his uncle had been filled with anger. Now he spoke as one who had considered the matter calmly and had reached a decision.

"The gods are now ready to make themselves known to our enemy," he continued. "Would you have one boy stand against them? His actions may cause the gods to delay a little longer."

"What makes you think that the gods are ready to act?" asked Ollin cautiously.

"Certain divinations have been made by the high priest of Huitzil," admitted Teteoni. "Our gods have been testing us to determine the depth of our loyalty. This is the final hour of testing. Today I was one of those called in council by the emperor Guatemozin. It was I who helped decide the fate of our people and our city."

"You mean about the surrender?" Ollin's voice was anxious. "I hope you counseled yes. It is hopeless to go on. It would be better to save those few of us who are left."

"You speak like an old woman!" cried Teteoni sharply. Chimal could imagine the fierce black eyes flashing in the scarred face. "The blood in your veins has turned to water, and it would have been better if Tecpatl had left you to die in the streets of Tenochtitlán."

"I do not love our enemy any more than you," argued Ollin. "But I have fought against them. I know their strength."

"Better, if need be, to give up our lives for our country than to drag them out in slavery among these foreigners," declared the high priest hotly. "If we should surrender, if we should bow to these white-skinned strangers from across the sea, they will tear down our altars and set up their own. When that happens Coatlique, Huitzil, Tlaloc, and all the other gods of Anahuac will leave. Their sacred fires will burn out, the sacrificial stones will become only slabs of gray rock, their use forgotten. And once they go, the gods will never return."

"Perhaps the time of which you speak is past," said Ollin quietly. "If they have not already gone, why have they not helped us before this?"

Chimal heard a rustle of straw as the priest rose to his feet.

"I will not stay to listen to such blasphemy. I am ashamed that one of my family should be so weak."

The following morning Guatemozin gave his answer to the demands of the Spaniards for surrender. Before daybreak, Aztecs poured through the gates of Tlaltelolco, attacking the enemy in their own camp. They were met by artillery and musketry fire that continued without stopping, and was aided by the cannon of the brigantine moored in that part of the lake. Sulfurous smoke grew so thick that before long it was impossible to see more than a few feet.

Chimal, armed with his *atatl*, was with the advancing horde, and with them fell back before the onslaught. Offense was useless. All they could do was to defend their homes, and this they did, fighting from rooftops, pouring down stones and arrows on the heads of those who systematically continued the destruction of the city.

Everyone had joined in the battle by this time. Slaves and women and children of the lowest class, who had not been included in Guatemozin's order to evacuate the city, helped by throwing stones from the flat rooftops. The toll of those who worked in the streets below was considerable, but when one of the enemy fell, there were two to take his place.

"You'll be sorry for what you're doing!" shouted Eecatl as he watched the foundation stones of a house across the street give way beneath the hammers of the enemy. "The more you tear down, the more you'll have to rebuild for us. For when we win, you shall be our slaves and work for us!"

"Fool," jeered the Tlascalan, wiping sweat from his face, "not to know that you have already lost! It is Malinche and his friends who have won."

"Friends today, slaves tomorrow!" cried Eecatl hotly as he fitted a fresh arrow to his bow. "Wait and see if I'm not right!"

At sundown the Spaniards and their allies halted the destruction for the night and retreated to their camp across the causeway.

"How much longer can it go on?" asked Eecatl wearily. "Surely the gods have tested us enough."

"It's because of that boy," declared a warrior who

had been fighting beside them. "The one who mocked the goddess. If he would give himself up, they would act."

Chimal heard him dully. Every bone and muscle in his body throbbed with pain, and for the last few hours he had been using his *atatl* blindly, hardly noticing where the stones fell. Now he came alive with sudden shock.

"What boy is that?" asked Eecatl.

"I forget his name," said the warrior. "But last night the priests came to the courtyard where we were sleeping and told us to be on the watch for such a boy. He has angered the gods, and until he is punished they will not help us."

"They didn't come to our courtyard." Eecatl yawned. "Perhaps he has been caught already."

"He cannot be taken yet, or the gods would make themselves known," decided the warrior. "The priests will come to your courtyard tonight. The homes of the traders, where we sleep, are many. It would take a long time to visit all of them."

Chimal stumbled along, automatically avoiding the boulders and rocks that choked the streets. What should he do? If the priests were right and his life was all that was needed to save what remained of Tenochtitlán, he should give himself up. But he couldn't believe that was so. The bloodthirsty gods had already received so many sacrifices, and it had made no difference to them. Besides, he was afraid.

They reached the house of Ollin, and Chimal looked up to the rooftop fearfully. No white cloth floated from the stairway leading down into the patio, and he turned in at the open gate.

"See you tomorrow, Chimal!" called Eecatl, continuing on.

It was strange, thought Chimal, that Tecpatl should allow the gate to stand ajar this way. It was an invitation for anyone to enter. The next moment he understood, but it was too late.

Strong arms had wrapped themselves around him, and his nose was filled with the familiar odors of the temple.

"That's the one!" cried Teteoni fiercely. "That is he who has made mockery of the Lady of the Skirt of Serpents, and insulted the gods of Anahuac. Bind him tightly and bring him to the temple."

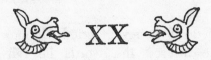

XX

"Are you sure he is dead?" asked Chimal for the hundredth time. He put his face close to the bars of the woven cage and peered out at the second cage, which held Tecpatl.

They had been confined all night, and during the dark hours they had found comfort in each other's voices. Now it was almost morning, and in the grayness shapes were taking form.

"At least I saw him fall," admitted Tecpatl. "When they caught me hanging out the white cloth as a warning to you, and dragged me down from the roof, your father came rushing from the room. He held his *maquahuitl* and would have defended me. But they struck him down."

"It's my fault," groaned Chimal. "If I hadn't saved Atototl from the gods, or if I had given myself up, my father would still be alive. And you wouldn't be here."

"Your father was glad you saved her," insisted Tecpatl in a troubled voice. "We had a long talk about it, he and I." He hesitated a moment while he looked up at the tall pyramid of Huitzil and Tezcatli, looming dark and foreboding in the early dawn. "And you must not blame yourself for him. It was his own words that brought about his death. He denied the gods!"

"Denied them?"

"He said he no longer believed in their power." The

stout cage moved slightly with Tecpatl's violent shudder. "And I listened to his blasphemy about the gods, which is why I am here. So you see, you are not to blame."

"Neither do I believe!" cried Chimal loudly. The moment he uttered the words he felt better. The thought must have been in the back of his mind for a long time, afraid to come forward, but with the knowledge that it was shared by his own father it became quite plain to him. "Except in Quetzal," he remembered. "Quetzal is a good god."

Tecpatl slumped to the bottom of his cage, moaning softly. Chimal could not persuade him to speak again.

In a few moments two priests came running down the winding stairs from the temple and began pulling and tugging at the cages.

"What are you doing?" cried Chimal.

"Is it time for the sacrifice?" asked Tecpatl. He had recovered from his fear, and now his voice was strong and clear.

"Your sacrifice to Coatlique must be delayed a little." One of the priests panted. "Our scouts report that the enemy is coming this way. Malinche thinks he will storm the temple, as he did in Tenochtitlán. But this time we are ready for him."

They pulled the two cages containing the prisoners up against the protecting side of the pyramid, away from the stairs. In that last minute Chimal saw that the temple grounds were filling with Guatemozin's warriors. They pushed their way through every gate, and many began mounting the steps to take battle stations on the flat terrace on top.

"Oh, for a *maquahuitl*," muttered Tecpatl, remembering the days before he had lost an arm. "If they would only turn me loose to fight, there might be a chance to redeem myself in the eyes of the gods!"

Before long, the battle began. Bursts of musketry pounded against Chimal's eardrums, and his nose was filled with the acrid smell of powder. He could hear shouts and whistles and groans, and the cage rocked occasionally as a gigantic boulder was pushed from the terrace to the courtyard. Protected as they were by the flaring side of the pyramid and the wall behind, they could see very little of what went on, but Chimal was sure that the Spaniards were attempting to gain the top. A moment later he knew that he had been right, for two combatants, locked in a hand-to-hand struggle, came tumbling through the air. They grazed the cage that held Tecpatl, causing it to fall crashing on its side.

"Tecpatl!" Chimal pressed his face against the bars. "Are you all right?"

For a long moment there was no answer; then there was the sound of splintering wood and Tecpatl crawled slowly out. He stood up, weaving a little in a dazed fashion, then walked over to the bodies of the two warriors.

Chimal saw him bend down and take the *maquahuitl* from the lifeless hand of the Aztec.

"Tecaptl!" he cried joyfully. "You're free. Now you can fight as you wanted to. Let me out, and I'll help you."

The one-armed man crossed over and stood next to the cage. Tears were running down his cheeks.

"I dare not, son of my dearest friend," he said sadly. "In my presence you denied the gods, just as your father did before you. They have taken him, and they will take you. Because I wished for a chance to redeem myself, Tezcatlipoco has seen fit to give it to me. If you pray to him, perhaps he will hear you too."

He turned and walked away, disappearing into the noise of battle around the corner of the pyramid, and Chimal stared after him. He yanked and pulled on the bars of his cage, although he knew it was useless. He had tried last night, and discovered that they would not move. Finally he sat down on the wooden floor, hopelessly awaiting the outcome of the battle.

It was not finished until late afternoon. By that time the ground around Chimal's cage was littered with boulders and the bodies of Aztecs and their enemies who had been hurled from the terrace atop the pyramid. Not one of them had touched the cage. It continued to stand unmolested, like a little island in a lake of destruction.

At first Chimal had braced himself, expecting each moment to hear that awful sound of splintering wood, to feel the heavy, crushing weight of man or rock. Then he began to wish that it would happen and put an end to the waiting. After that he grew numb, and the deafening sounds of war became part of an awful dream, a nightmare, from which he could not awaken.

When they stopped, the silence was startling. For a moment Chimal wondered which side had triumphed; then he reminded himself that it didn't matter. He was the enemy of both sides.

After a time the animal-shaped headdress of a Tlascalan appeared around the corner of the pyramid. Chimal heard the shrill whistle as the man alerted his comrades to more bodies to be searched for loot. He closed his eyes, telling himself that the *maquahuitl* of a Tlascalan was no worse than the knife of a priest.

They saw the cage immediately, and he could hear

them clustering all around, laughing and talking with each other. He could smell their breath and the odors from their bodies, and he felt their hands poking through the bars and jabbing into his body. Then, because he did not want to be accused of cowardice by one of the hated Tlascalans, he forced himself to open his eyes, and at the same moment he heard a deeper voice speaking from the outskirts of the crowd.

The Tlascalans snarled, but stepped back, making room for a Spaniard. He was not one of the great lords, for he wore the padded jacket of the common soldier and leather boots that came up to his thighs. But he had the respect of the Tlascalans, who allowed him plenty of room.

The Spaniard bent over, forcing his bearded face below the metal helmet close against the bars. The next moment he grinned in recognition.

"Why, it's Orteguilla's friend!" he exclaimed. "The boy who used to come to the palace. Why are you in here playing bird-in-a-cage?"

Chimal stared back at the bearded face, recognizing Bernal Díaz, one of the men who had often served as guard at the palace gates.

"I'm to be sacrificed to the gods," he explained weakly.

Díaz frowned with disapproval as he unlocked the cage door.

"There'll be no more sacrifices," he declared gruffly. "They've just tumbled the two idols off the top of the pyramid, and as soon as we finish burning the heathen temples we'll be off for camp. I think I'll just take you along."

XXI

"I wish you wouldn't watch," said Orteguilla. "It will be over soon."

"But they're my people," insisted Chimal sadly. "And that's my home that is being destroyed."

"It's too bad about your home," agreed Orteguilla. "It was nice, at least as much as I could see of it that day you hid me in the warehouse. But your people turned against you. They wanted to kill you. I don't see how you can be sorry for them, especially since they have no one to blame but their own stubbornness. They should have given up long ago."

Chimal did not answer. There was no use trying to explain how he felt to Orteguilla.

He had been a prisoner of the Spaniards for over a week, and when Cortés had heard that he had been taken from a cage where he awaited sacrifice he had said that the boy did not need to be restrained. No one in his right mind would return voluntarily to such a fate. Besides, Chimal, because of his knowledge of the Spanish tongue, would be of value later, and must be well treated now. He slept on the ground at night, shared the soldiers' food, and spent his days with Father Olmedo. Early mornings and evenings, there was Orteguilla to talk with, and Chimal plied him with questions. The page served as messenger between the leaders and the troops, so he knew what was going on.

The destruction had continued, and all that remained of Tlaltelolco was a single canal and the section that contained the homes and warehouses of the merchants. This morning, aided by a stiff breeze that filled their sails, the brigantines had collected to begin the final devastation of this area.

Chimal had seen their white shapes through the grayness of pre-dawn, gathering like thunder caps above a mountain. Now, with their cannon trained on the wharfs and warehouses, they were destroying the last stronghold of the Aztecs. His stomach writhed at the knowledge of what was going on behind that dense screen of smoke.

"I have to go," said Orteguilla uncomfortably. "God willing, I'll see you tonight, Chimal. And if I were you I wouldn't watch. It only makes you feel worse."

Chimal nodded miserably. He knew that Orteguilla was right. He ought to go to the other end of the camp, away from this place that overlooked the lake, but he couldn't tear himself away.

In mid-morning he was joined by Father Olmedo. The priest gathered up his robes and sat down on the ground beside the boy.

"It is very sad to see one's home being destroyed," he said compassionately. "But there will be another home someday."

"Not like this one," insisted Chimal.

"No. A better home. A Christian home." Father Olmedo missed no opportunity to press his faith. "Someday, Chimal, that city on the lake will rise again. The homes will be rebuilt, but not the heathen temples. Instead there will be great cathedrals, dedicated to the true God, a God of lovingkindness."

"Like Quetzal," repeated Chimal stubbornly. He was willing to deny the bloodthirsty deity, but the old god Quetzal remained very close to his heart.

"It will take time, time," said Father Olmedo with a sigh. After a moment he looked again at the billowing smoke across the lake. "I wonder where the people went. I hope there was some refuge they could find."

"They've gone to the market," said Chimal positively.

Although it had been laid low by the Spaniards, there was no place else for them to go. Custom was strong, and it was to the market in Tlaltelolco that people always went. He could almost see them in his mind's eye. The arcades lining the great paved square, which had once been filled with splendid wares, would now be crowded with frightened people. There they would stay, huddled together in their starving misery, until the cannons on the brigantines were still.

"Terrible, terrible," said Father Olmedo sorrowfully.

"If there was just some way I could help them!" cried Chimal. "If there was only something I could do!"

Father Olmedo shook his shaven head sadly. He had no suggestions.

Finally the cannon stopped firing.

"It is over," said Father Olmedo gently. "Shall we go?"

But Chimal wanted to stay. Smoke hung over the water, obscuring the opposite shore line, and he wanted to see for himself. Perhaps, like his cage in the battle at the temple, some dear landmark had been spared.

Before that could happen, Atototl joined them on the bank. She was alone, and tears were running down her face.

"My child," chided Father Olmedo, "you should not be here. You should have stayed with Doña Marina."

"But she is gone, Father," explained Atototl. "They came for her. They have captured the emperor Guatemozin as he tried to flee from the city. Malinche has gone to receive his surrender. It will be on the pyramid at Tlaltelolco, in sight of all the people. And Doña Marina went to act as the interpreter."

Chimal stood up. He felt as though a heavy weight had been lifted from him. Orteguilla had been right after all; it was over. Without a leader, the Aztecs would lay down their arms. Perhaps he should be grieving at the Spanish victory, but all he could think of was that the useless slaughter was at an end. Now the hungry people could find food. He looked at Father Olmedo with anxious eyes.

"Now surely there must be some way I can help my people."

"I'm certain there will be," agreed the priest. "And God will show it to you."

Guatemozin asked for permission to lead the remnants of his people from their ruined city, and the exodus began the following morning.

Chimal stood with the soldiers guarding the end of the causeway, over which the refugees must pass. It was a chill, damp day, and even in the padded surcoat that Orteguilla had lent him, his teeth chattered.

Last night the basin encircled by its mountain range had rocked with a storm such as he had never seen.

215

Thunder had crashed overhead, and the sound had been thrown back in echoes between the giant peaks. Lightning flashed, flooding the valley in dazzling sheets of bluish-white, while rain fell in such torrents that it stood upon the ground in deep pools. The wind, swirling in eddies and roaring in unabated fury, had sounded like the voices of threatening gods.

Chimal had slept very little, but he knew that the people huddled in the barren flats of Tlaltelolco had slept even less. That was probably what was making them so late arriving at the causeway.

The guards were cross and ill-tempered.

"We should have finished them off when we had the chance," growled one of them. "Cortés asked too much, expecting us to stand here all day like a flock of sheep. Their treasure's gone. What good are these people to us?"

"They'll work the mines and bring out more treasure," answered another wisely. "Cortés is planning to open new mines, and he'll need many men. This is only the beginning."

Chimal shut his lips tightly, holding back an angry remark, but his eyes peered anxiously across the long stone causeway. Why didn't they come? Had they all been struck by one of those terrible bolts of lightning in the storm?

It was mid-morning before the beginning of the procession appeared at the opposite end of the causeway. They advanced slowly, and it seemed to Chimal that they scarcely crept along. In the advance were Guatemozin and twenty nobles, all that remained of the once numerous Aztec aristocracy. They were stripped of all their finery, and wore only simple cotton garments, but their heads were still high, their emaciated frames erect.

Chimal fell on his knees as the emperor came near, his tear-filled eyes upon the ground. But when he heard the voice of one of the guards speak sharply, disrespectfully, he looked up.

"Move on. Faster, you miserable heathen! Do you expect us to stand here all day, while you take your time?"

Guatemozin stopped. He did not understand the words, but there was no mistaking the tone.

"My people are weak from starvation and wounds," he announced calmly. "They can scarcely walk. We cannot hurry. But Malinche has promised that we may all go free."

"You don't expect me to understand that heathen gibberish," declared the guard scornfully. "Move on. Hurry it up!"

Chimal's face flushed at the insult to his emperor. He stood up and walked over to the guard.

"His Majesty says that the people cannot walk any faster," he said angrily. "They are sick and starving. And Cortés ordered that they are to be allowed to cross over."

The face of the guard darkened with anger, but the others began to laugh.

"He's telling the truth, Juan," reminded one of them. "They'll come as fast as they can, knowing there's food at the end. Tell Guatemozin to make it as fast as he can, boy."

Obediently Chimal turned to his emperor, but he remembered to keep his eyes turned down.

"The soldier says he understands that the people cannot walk fast, Your Majesty," he said. "But, as you

know, the land beyond is green from the rainy season. There will be food for all, once they have left the city."

"Move on," ordered Guatemozin, and at first Chimal did not understand that the emperor was speaking to his nobles. It was only when the sandaled feet and thin brown legs stepped to one side, out of the way of the procession, that he realized that he himself was being singled out.

"What is your name?" asked Guatemozin. "And how does it happen that you speak the language of our conquerors?"

"My name is Chimalpopoca." His voice sounded very small, even to himself. "And while I was at the *calmecac*, I went every day to the Palace of Axaya' as a spy. I learned the language there."

"I remember now," said Guatemozin. "Your father is Ollin, the trader. He served us well, and so did you. Perhaps you can continue to serve."

"Anything, Your Majesty!" cried Chimal fervently. For a moment he forgot himself and looked directly at his monarch. He had a glimpse of thoughtful dark eyes in a thin, proud face before he remembered to look back at the ground.

"We are a vanquished people," admitted Guatemozin. "As such, our own language will fall into disuse, and we must learn that of our conquerors. Until that happens we will need an interpreter. Perhaps you can serve us in that way."

"Oh, I will, I will!" cried Chimal joyfully. "I will come to you as soon as I can. I don't think they will keep me a prisoner now that it is over."

"No," agreed Guatemozin. "I think Malinche will see your value as a teacher to your people."

Chimal remembered suddenly.

"But perhaps the people will not want me," he confessed sadly. "My uncle, who was high priest to Coatlique, said I insulted the goddess. He said that only my sacrifice would satisfy her."

"The gods of Anahuac are gone." Guatemozin's voice was expressionless. "The priests said that they left last night, and that they will never return. Their farewells were heard in the voices of the storm that swept the valley. Malinche has said that we must worship his god now, and the god of the white-skinned strangers does not call for sacrifices."

Chimal was silent. He was safe, and Atototl was safe. They could return to the Aztecs whenever they pleased, but he was not sure that he would be entirely welcome. Not at first. He had cheated the old gods, while they were still here, and he would have to earn the respect of his people all over again. It would not be easy.

Guatemozin must have read his thoughts, for when he spoke again, his voice was kind.

"Stay here, at the end of the causeway," he ordered. "As our people cross, encourage them to continue on. They are weak and sick. Each step is torture. Remind them of the open hills, rich with food, that are just ahead, of the fresh, sweet water that is there to drink. Tell them that their emperor awaits their coming. And speak gently. Many are without hope, and if you can give them that, this moment will dwell longer in their minds than all your former wrongdoing."

"I will," promised Chimal fervently. "I'll stay here until the last one is on his way. Then I'll beg Malinche's permission to come to you myself."

He turned from his emperor to the pitiful procession straggling across the causeway. And as he spoke to them, many raised their eyes from the wet stones underfoot to the lush green hills that stretched ahead and found the strength to totter on.

AUTHOR'S NOTE

Tenochtitlán, now Mexico City, was rebuilt by the Spaniards, using native slave labor, after the conquest, but never back to its original state. The canals were never cleared, but gradually covered over with many feet of soil. The temple pyramids were flattened to the ground, until only the Hill of Chapultepec rises above the level city. The forests surrounding the area were denuded of timber, and the lakes dried up until little trace of them now remains.

The Zocalco, or main plaza, was erected on the site of Montezuma's palace and the Great Temple, and the Spaniards used some of the remains of these structures when they built the present cathedral and national palace. Here also are the ruins of an ancient Aztec structure believed to have been part of the Great Temple. It includes a carved snake head, said to have been one of those surmounting the wall around the Great Pyramid. In the National Museum the calendar stone may be seen, and part of the aqueduct that fed the royal fountains from the springs of Chapultepec still remains.

It took Cortés only seventy-five days from the time he launched his brigantines to conquer the city. The losses of the Aztecs during that last siege are estimated at between a hundred and twenty thousand to two hundred and forty thousand. How many survivors there were is not known, but it took three days for all of them to cross the causeway into the open country beyond.

The prophecy of Eecatl that the former allies of the Spaniards would become their vassals, along with the Aztecs, came true, and all of Mexico remained under Spanish rule for three centuries. A revolution in 1810 resulted in the overthrowing of their hated conquerors. But there still remains much of the Spanish influence in Mexico: the language, the high-ceilinged colonial architecture, the beautiful cathedrals, and the religion that Father Olmedo brought from across the sea.

The few remaining sacrificial altars are now only carved stones in museums, and the fragments of stone idols are but hideous mementos of another day, for the gods of Anahuac, who fled on the night of August 13, 1521, never returned.

BIBLIOGRAPHY

Daily Life of the Aztecs, by Jacques Soustelle. Translated from the French by P. O'Brian. London, England: Weidenfeld & Nicolson, 1955.

History of the Conquest of Mexico, by William H. Prescott. Philadelphia, Pennsylvania: David McKay, 1843.

The Aztecs, People of the Sun, by Alfonso Caso. Translated by Lowell Dunham. Norman, Oklahoma: University of Oklahoma Press, 1958.

Ancient Civilizations of Mexico and Central America, by Herbert J. Spinden. New York, New York: The American Museum of Natural History Anthropological Handbook Fund, 1949.

Aztecs of Mexico, by George C. Vaillant. New York, New York: The American Museum of Natural History Science Series, 1941. Revised edition, Doubleday & Company, Inc., Garden City, New York: 1962.

GLOSSARY

The rules for the pronunciation of Aztec names are really quite simple. *X* generally has a *sh* sound; *qu* has a *k* value; *hu* and *gu* have a *w* sound when preceding a vowel.

Acamapichtli	a young slave boy
Anahuac	the geographical part of Mexico in which the Aztecs lived
Atatls	weapons used for hurling darts and stones
Atolli	maize porridge
Atototl	a thirteen-year-old Aztec girl, sister of Chimal
Axayacatl or Axaya'	the palace named after a great emperor who preceded Montezuma II; used by the Spaniards
Cacama	Lord of Tezcuco
Calmecac	the school for priests
Chapultepec	"Hill of Grasshoppers"—Montezuma's summer palace; from here came water for the city
Chimalpopoca or Chimal	an eleven-year-old Aztec boy
Chinampas	the wandering islands upon which Tenochtitlán had been built
Cholula	the Aztec holy city, whose people followed Cortez and helped form his return army

Cipactli	a slave owned by Ollin, Chimal's father
Citlalcoatl	a physician-priest at the Great Temple
Coacalo	the temple in Tenochtitlán where the gods of conquered cities resided
Coatlique	Lady of the Skirt of Serpents: earth goddess, associated with spring; mother of the sun, moon, and stars
Cortés, Hernán	the leader of the Spanish army; called *Malinche* by the Aztecs
Cuitlahua	Lord of Iztapalapan; Montezuma's brother
Doña Marina	the interpreter for Cortés; her native Aztec name had been Malinche
Don Pedro Alvarado	lieutenant to Cortés; called *Tonatiuh* by the Aztecs
Eecatl	an Aztec boy, friend of Chimal
Father Olmedo	one of two priests with the Spanish expedition
Guatemozin	nephew of the emperor, Montezuma II
Huitzilopochtli	the god of war and sun, chief god or patron of Tenochtitlán
Ichpochtlaque	the school for young girls, attended by Chimal's sister, Atototl
Itzocans	a tribe that followed Cortés and helped form his return army
Iyac	the haircut of a soldier who has taken his first prisoner: the hair in the back is cut, and the hair grown to fall over the right ear
Iztaccihuatl	"The white woman"—a volcanic mountain
Iztapalapan	one of the great dikes stretching across Lake Tezcuco to the city gates of Tenochtitlán

Iztlilton	one of the gods of healing
Maquahuitl	a small wooden sword with obsidian blade
Maxtlatl	a loincloth
Mazatl	Chimal's mother
Montezuma II	emperor of the Aztecs
Ocelotl	a warrior-teacher
Ollin	an Aztec merchant; Chimal's father
Orteguilla	a young Spanish page to Montezuma II
Otomies	a neighboring tribe of the Aztecs, living between Anahuac and Tlascala
Panache	a plumed headdress worn by nobility
Piochtli	the formal haircut designating a student: the hair is cut short except for a single long lock on the nape of the neck
Pochteca	the name for a traveling trader or merchant
Popocatepetl	a volcano
Quauhpopoca	a tribal chief
Quauhtli	a student at the school for priests; Chimal's friend
Quetzalcoatl	the god of wind, life, and morning; credited with teaching Aztecs science, weaving, and art
Tecpatl	the aide to Ollin, Chimal's father
Telpochcalli	the young men's school for warriors
Tenochtitlán	a major city in Mexico; home of Montezuma II and the location of this story— now Mexico City
Tepeacans	a tribe that followed Cortés and helped form his return army
Teteoni	the high priest in the Temple of Coatlique; Chimal's uncle

Tezcatlipoco	the god of the smoking mirror, of war and destruction; patron god of Tlaltelolco
Tezcuco	a lake surrounding Tenochtitlán; also the name of a neighboring city
Tianquez	the market
Tilmatli	a cotton cloak
Tlacateotl	a captain in Guatemozin's army
Tlacopan	one of several causeways entering Tenochtitlán
Tlaloc	the rain god with the power of thunder and lightning; god of growing things, hence, god of farmers
Tlaltelolco	a suburb of Tenochtitlán, in which Chimal and his family lived, and which contained the great market
Tlascalans	natives of a tribe hostile to the Aztecs
Tlazolteotl	the goddess who devours an Aztec's evildoing in return for a penance; called "goddess who eats filth"
Tochtli	a maid in Chimal's home
Tonatiuh	the sun god; the Aztec name for Pedro Alvarado because of his blond hair and beard
Tzapotlatenan	one of the goddesses of healing
Xochimilco	the city in the fresh-water lagoon which fed the great salt lake, Tezcuco
Xocotl	one of Ollin's slaves
Yacatecuhtli	the god of merchants

ABOUT THE AUTHOR

The mother of two daughters, Evelyn Sibley Lampman is a graduate of Oregon State College and was Educational Director of the Portland, Oregon, NBC radio station for a number of years. Several of her radio scripts have won national awards, and her stories have appeared in many popular magazines.

With equal storytelling skill, Mrs. Lampman has written intriguing fantasies as well as fascinating historical novels and biographies. Her first book for young people was published in 1948, and since then, fortunately for her devoted readers, she has written more than one book a year. Mrs. Lampman's other titles are listed in the front of this book.